He was leaning toward her slightly, one hand over the back of the stall, the other free to do whatever it wanted.

She suddenly wanted his arms around her. She suddenly wanted a lot more than that.

As if he was reading the message in her eyes, he murmured, "I almost did this last night."

And then his arm was around her and he bent his head to hers.

The first touch of Zack's lips wasn't anything like Jenny expected. She'd expected hard, possessive and arrogant. His lips were firm as if he knew what he wanted. But they were coaxing, too... encouraging her to respond.

If she had thought further than that, she might have saved them both a lot of trouble. But she didn't, because all of her concentration was on the feel of his mouth, the touch of his tongue against hers, the strength of his arms as he pulled her closer. The kiss was a flash from the past that could be a plunge into the future.

Dear Reader,

Can a woman ever forget her first love? Fortunately, my first love proposed! He was my first serious relationship and we clicked as if we'd known each other before we met. We fit.

Zack and Jenny fit when they found each other as teenagers. But dreams and past hurts separated them.... Until fifteen years later, at their high school reunion, they realized they still had a bond that might never fade.

This book celebrates young love and the reuniting of hearts. To young love, mature love and the love in between!

Best,

Karen Rose Smith

ONCE UPON
A GROOM

KAREN ROSE SMITH

Harlequin®

SPECIAL EDITION

Recycling programs
for this product may
not exist in your area.

ISBN-13: 978-0-373-65628-8

ONCE UPON A GROOM

Copyright © 2011 by Karen Rose Smith

All rights reserved. Except for use in any review, the reproduction or utilization of this work in whole or in part in any form by any electronic, mechanical or other means, now known or hereafter invented, including xerography, photocopying and recording, or in any information storage or retrieval system, is forbidden without the written permission of the publisher, Harlequin Enterprises Limited, 225 Duncan Mill Road, Don Mills, Ontario M3B 3K9, Canada.

This is a work of fiction. Names, characters, places and incidents are either the product of the author's imagination or are used fictitiously, and any resemblance to actual persons, living or dead, business establishments, events or locales is entirely coincidental.

This edition published by arrangement with Harlequin Books S.A.

For questions and comments about the quality of this book please contact us at Customer_eCare@Harlequin.ca.

® and TM are trademarks of Harlequin Books S.A., used under license. Trademarks indicated with ® are registered in the United States Patent and Trademark Office, the Canadian Trade Marks Office and in other countries.

www.Harlequin.com

Printed in U.S.A.

Books by Karen Rose Smith

KAREN ROSE SMITH

is the award-winning, bestselling novelist of more than seventy published romances. Her latest series, Reunion Brides, is set near Flagstaff, Arizona, in Miners Bluff, the fictional town she created. After visiting Flagstaff, the Grand Canyon and Sedona, she felt that the scenery was so awe-inspiring that she had to set books there. When not writing, she likes to garden, growing herbs, vegetables and flowers. She lives with her husband—her college sweetheart—and their two cats in Pennsylvania. Readers may email her through her website at www.karenrosesmith.com, follow her on Facebook or Twitter @karenrosesmith or write to her at P.O. Box 1545, Hanover, PA 17331.

With fond remembrance of Joan.

Prologue

July

As Zack Decker approached Jenny Farber in the cafeteria, decorated with blue and yellow streamers, memories washed over him. He struggled to maintain the cool facade that had enabled him to direct the most temperamental actresses...that had allowed him to hide the turmoil that had churned inside him since he'd left Miners Bluff fifteen years ago.

In a strapless yellow dress that accentuated her slim but curvy figure, Jenny was dancing with a classmate. The way she was smiling up at the man lit the wrong fuse on Zack's usually controlled temper.

He clasped Brody Hazlett's shoulder, dredged up a smile he didn't feel and ignored the hushed surprise of other classmates he hadn't seen in years. "Can I cut in?"

Brody let go of Jenny's hand and faced Zack, his expression friendly. "Hi, Zack. It's good to see you. The reunion must have meant a lot to you."

"The reunion, and a few other things," Zack said off-handedly, his gaze on Jenny as the silver disco ball spun, casting flickering lights across her heart-shaped face. She'd left a message on his cell phone last week. He remembered her words. *Zack, please come home for the reunion. I need to talk to you about Silas's health.*

And here he was.

Taking Jenny's hand in his, he circled her with his arm and steeled himself. As his hand brushed over the bare skin of her back, golden sparks lit her expressive brown eyes, bringing back too many buried memories.

"How long can you stay?" Jenny always went straight for the bottom line.

"Until tomorrow afternoon. I have to be on location in England on Monday."

"That's all the time you can spare?" Her voice was less accusatory than wistful...or regretful.

"I hadn't intended to come to the reunion, but with your call, I revamped my schedule."

The rhythm of the music overtook them for a few moments. It was a nineties ballad he recalled too well. The melody had wafted from the radio in the hayloft as the two of them...

He shut down the movie in his mind, leaned away from her slender body that had caused an instantaneous and powerful reaction in his. "Do you want to go somewhere quieter to talk?"

Quickly glancing around, she motioned toward the shadowy corridor lined with lockers where they had once exchanged heartfelt secrets...and kisses.

He led the way as he always had, trying to forget that fifteen years ago, she hadn't followed.

Jenny attempted to calm her racing pulse and swallowed hard. Being in Zack's arms again upturned her world until she became almost dizzy! He *couldn't* still do that to her. She wouldn't let him.

She watched him stride toward the corridor leading to the stairwell where he stopped and waited for her. He obviously wasn't used to waiting for anyone. He'd left her behind once before. She imagined he wouldn't hesitate to do it again.

Remember, he asked you to go with him.

Yes, he had. But she'd been eighteen and had finally found roots with Zack's parents. As for Zack, he'd wanted to escape both his roots and his mom and dad. All he'd focused on were his dreams and a film school scholarship in L.A. She hadn't been able to pin their future on something so intangible. Her own father's dreams had disappointed her too many times to count. Her job as a groom at the Rocky D, Olivia Decker's faith in her and Silas Decker's promise to give her more responsibility in the future had been grounding forces much more powerful than her fear of what lay ahead with Zack.

But she *had* loved him in the ferocious way only an eighteen-year-old could love.

As she walked beside Zack, her high heels clicking on the waxed tile, her arm brushed his. The shiver that rippled through her almost loosened the mass of blond curls she'd pinned on top of her head. How could the brush of her skin against his suit jacket cause such a reaction?

He stopped halfway down the corridor, obviously hoping for privacy.

She gazed up at Zack, reminded again of how tall six-foot-two could be, how broad his shoulders had become, how slim his hips still were. He'd always oozed a James Dean kind of sensuality and that hadn't changed. With a small cleft at the center of his jaw, his tousled, almost raven-black hair just barely tamed by an obviously expensive cut, his stormy-blue eyes, she realized the tabloids always got it right—he *was* a heart-breaker.

But then, she knew that from personal experience.

She felt tongue-tied with him, and he seemed to be at a similar loss for words until he said, "I spoke with Dad when I arrived. Sorry I missed you, but I was delayed."

Had father and son finally had a heart-to-heart and found common ground? "And?" she prompted, instead of saying what she was thinking.

"And," he drawled, "I don't understand why you needed me to come. He's as contentious as ever. He wanted to know if I flew all this way for a few dances for old times' sake."

"What did you tell him?"

"The truth—that you thought something was wrong with him."

"Oh, Zack, you didn't! I wanted you to observe him when he wasn't aware of it. If he knows you're watching, he'll act all macho."

"Jenny, I don't have time to follow him around and act as if I'm not. Like he wouldn't catch on to *that* in about ten minutes."

Men! She was ready to throttle the two of them.

Zack hadn't been home for eight years—not since his mother's funeral.

"Something is wrong with him," she insisted with so much vehemence, loose tendrils of hair fluttered along her cheeks. "He can't walk from the house through the barn without getting winded. He hasn't taken Hercules riding in weeks. He doesn't even watch me train anymore. I spent every day in that house with him for the past sixteen years and I know when he's off his game. He's off, Zack, and I think there's a physical reason."

"Then make him a doctor's appointment."

"I did, several times. He won't go. A few days before, he always cancels it."

Zack blew out a long breath and looked as if he were drawing on a short store of patience. "What do you want from me, Jenny?"

The first answer that came to mind was—*Not a blasted thing.* Then she remembered the manners Olivia had taught her...the wisdom that she'd get what she wanted more easily with a light touch than with a heavy one.

"Silas is getting older. What I think he needs most from you is your forgiveness."

They both went silent, then the surprise on Zack's face quickly faded. "What do you want me to forgive him for?" he asked, in a low but angry voice. "For the gambling and drinking? For the affairs that hurt my mom? For his lack of faith in my abilities and my career path? Or for the big one—for being responsible for my mother's death?"

Jenny barely opened her mouth to protest before Zack moved closer. "Don't give me a sympathetic, 'Oh, Zack, that's not true.' Her plane went down because of a storm, but she was on it because my father had driven her away."

Jenny had been in the barn that day when Olivia had confronted Silas, holding the credit card statement showing the hotel bill, and the flower order she'd never received. Half the ranch hands had overheard their argument.

All Jenny could say was, "He's a different man now."

"Different? He's the same man he's always been. So what if he doesn't gamble anymore?"

This might be her only chance to make Zack understand. "When he lost Olivia, he didn't just lose his wife, he lost *you.* All of that changed him."

Zack shook his head. "You're as naive as you've ever been."

The arrogance in Zack's voice nettled her. "No, I'm not naive, but I've watched him and worked beside him every day for all these years. He's changed. He not only doesn't gamble, but he doesn't drink, either."

Instead of responding, Zack peered down the hall to the reunion going strong in the cafeteria. Then very quietly, firmly, he insisted, "I don't belong here, Jenny. You fit in better than I ever did. My father didn't want a son who escaped his parents' fights by videotaping the scenery on Moonshadow Mountain, by recreating an old Western with some of his friends in Horsethief Canyon."

Tears burned her eyes because he was right. Zack and Silas had never understood each other very well. Still, she answered his vehemence with softness. "Silas wanted a son to take over the Rocky D. That's all he ever expected of you."

"You know I loved training the horses, almost as

much as you did. But I never wanted this to be the extent of my world. I had bigger dreams than that."

"And you've made them come true."

After a lengthy pause, he responded, "Yes, I have."

She heard the pride in his voice and knew his success was as important to him as the Rocky D was to Silas. "Then be a little generous," she pleaded. "Be kind, and forgive what neither of you can change. Find out what it is to be father and son as grown-ups."

"You're still an optimist who won't step outside of her little world."

"Don't talk down to me," she returned hotly. "I found the life I want in Miners Bluff. If you want to travel the world, be my guest. But I'm perfectly happy right here on the Rocky D."

"You're like him," Zack maintained. "You both have tunnel vision. The two of you believe the Rocky D is the only world that matters, but you're wrong. You're also wrong about Dad needing my forgiveness. Granted, I haven't been in much contact with him since Mom died—I phone now and then because he *is* my father— but he's *never* reached out to me."

If her plea was for herself, she'd let Zack walk away. But it was for Silas. "Please, Zack. Can't you at least stay for a few days? Or at least come back after the shoot."

"The shoot will take three months."

The walls in Zack's eyes were as solid as the armor he wore on his heart. "So why did you bother to come home?"

"Because you asked, and so I could get a quick peek for myself. I think you're overreacting. Dad might simply be growing older and you don't want to recognize that."

"You're wrong."

"Time will tell. Make him another doctor's appointment. That's all you can do."

"He might listen to you."

"To a son he's never listened to before? I doubt that."

"You're as stubborn and blind as he is!" Her voice had risen and she hoped it hadn't carried down the hall.

"I'm not going to argue with you, Jenny. I have a plane to catch tomorrow afternoon."

She was outraged that he cared so little about Silas and the Rocky D that he wouldn't stay long enough to see the full picture.

"This project is important to me," he went on. "It has to get off to a good start."

"And you don't care what ends *here?*"

"Everything here ended for me a long time ago." With those words, and a last long look, Zack walked away.

Jenny stared at his back, remembering the first time he'd left her. Six weeks later, she'd discovered she was pregnant. Six weeks after that, she'd miscarried.

Zack Decker might think he knew everything, but he still didn't know *that*.

Chapter One

Late October

Finally back in L.A., Zack studied the stack of script revisions on his desk, the mound of messages not important enough to return while he'd been on location. He started with the most recent, saw Dawson Barrett's name and smiled. He and Dawson had kept in touch over the years, and they'd reconnected briefly at the reunion a few months ago.

He'd call Dawson when he returned to his penthouse later that night. From the amount of reading on his desk, he would be staying in the city this weekend.

He swore. He'd been looking forward to a couple of days at his house in Malibu. That was the one place he could relax. Usually he derived satisfaction and a sense of accomplishment after a movie was in the can. But this time, his mind had kept drifting. The adrenaline rush had been missing and he didn't know why.

His cell phone vibrated against his hip. He considered ignoring it, then pulled it from his belt and studied the caller ID on the screen, surprised to see it was Jenny. A sense of foreboding zipped from his head to his loafers.

"Jenny?"

Words came tumbling from her. "I was afraid you'd still be out of the country."

"I just got back yesterday. What's wrong?"

He heard her take a steadying breath and he braced himself for what was coming.

"Silas collapsed. I rode with him in the ambulance to Flagstaff—" Her voice caught.

Zack went numb, absolutely numb. Images of his dad riding Hercules, giving the hands orders, smoking a Cuban cigar, flew through his mind. The idea of Silas being loaded into an ambulance... How could Jenny have been so right when he'd seen no evidence of a problem? *Was* he blind where his father was concerned?

He pushed out the words lodged in his throat. "I'll catch the first flight out."

"Zack..."

To his surprise, he still felt connected to Jenny and could read her thoughts. "I know you're scared. Try to take a deep breath and hope for the best. Call me with updates. If I'm on the plane, I'll get your message when I land."

"What if you can't get a seat?"

"Then I'll charter a plane. You don't have to go through this alone."

"Thank you."

Her voice wobbled in a way that was so unlike Jenny that Zack's throat tightened. "No thanks necessary. I should have listened to you."

She said nothing.

"I'll be there as soon as I can. Hold tight."

She murmured her thanks again and ended the call.

Conflicting emotions battered Zack as he turned to his computer to make a reservation. What would he find when he got to Flagstaff? *Hope for the best,* he'd told Jenny.

Just what *was* the best?

Late that night, Zack rushed into the emergency room entrance of the stucco and brick hospital in Flagstaff, his pulse racing. He'd thought he'd distanced himself from his father. He'd thought he simply didn't care anymore. Maybe that's why he hadn't seen the symptoms Jenny had noticed when he'd been home for the reunion. Or maybe his father pretended as much as he himself did.

It was possible his father had put up a front for Zack's benefit, but Zack's coolness and reserve toward Silas wasn't a pretense. They'd had many arguments before Zack had left for film school. Growing up, he'd often seen his dad inebriated after a high-stakes poker game. He'd heard his parents' arguments and known his dad was always at the root of them. When Zack had learned what had happened the day his mother died, why she'd taken off in that airplane to visit her sister in Montana, he'd disowned his father just as his father had practically disowned him when he left the ranch to pursue a film career.

After inquiring at the desk and showing ID, he headed for the cardiac intensive care unit and found Jenny in one of the waiting rooms. Even looking distraught and pale, she was a beautiful woman. At thirty-three, maturity had touched her in attractive ways. Her glossy blond, shoulder-length hair framed a heart-shaped face that had taken on a more haunting beauty. Her deep brown eyes, always wide with emotions, were stunning as she looked up at him.

"I'm so glad you're here. They've stabilized him but—" The quick shutdown of her thoughts told Zack just how upset she was.

Shrugging out of his leather jacket, he laid it over the back of the sofa.

"Did you even have time to pack?" she asked.

"No. I keep a duffle in my office with a change of clothes and workout gear. I just grabbed that."

"Are you going to try to see him now?"

"Yes, for a few minutes. Thanks for giving me his doctor's number. I called him after I landed. He said he'd noted on the chart that I could see him when I arrived."

"Zack, you *can't* upset him." She looked as if that was hard for her to say, but yet she knew she had to say it.

Her regret didn't help the sting, though, and he replied, almost angrily, "Do you think I would? My God, Jenny, I don't wish him harm."

"How would I know what you wish him, Zack?"

She was right. How would she know? They hadn't really talked except about the most mundane practical things when he called his father now and then. He'd felt it was his duty to keep in touch even though he hadn't wanted to. Sometimes Jenny would answer. Sometimes they'd exchange pleasantries. Others she'd just tell Silas he was on the line.

We live in different worlds, he reminded himself, not for the first time. Yet standing here, facing her again, years dropped away and lingering nudges of what they'd once shared startled him. Memories ran through his head of the two of them sitting on the corral fence talking...of gentling a foal together...of graduating... of making love in the hayloft. No—not making love. Having sex. If it had been love, Jenny would have gone with him to L.A. when he'd asked her.

"How long are you going to stay?" she asked, and he could see she was already preparing herself for the fact he might be here merely twenty-four hours again.

"I don't know. Let's just see what happens after tomorrow. I'll conference with the doctor and then decide."

She appeared to want to say something, maybe ask him if he could stay longer than a day, but she didn't. Instead she murmured, "I'll get a blanket and pillows while you're gone. I'm bunking here tonight."

Zack knew his father had become a dad to Jenny, the way her own had never been. It was ironic that Silas couldn't be a real father to Zack when Zack was growing up, but with Jenny—Silas Decker had never been anything but supportive, positive and encouraging with her even before his wife had died. Maybe that's because Jenny hadn't been a disappointment to him. Or because she had stepped into the role that Zack had been groomed for but had refused.

"I'm going to see him now." Zack steeled himself

for the visit, knowing he did have to distance himself from this experience and whatever happened next.

Surprising him, Jenny crossed to him and touched his forearm. It was just a whisper of a touch, no pressure at all. Yet Zack felt the fire of it. He felt his body respond to it, and he pulled away before she could guess what was happening. But not before he saw the disappointment on her face that they couldn't have a heart-to-heart about this.

There would be no heart-to-hearts, not tonight, not in the days to come. He didn't do that because letting himself be vulnerable would only invite pain. He'd seen it with his parents. He'd felt it with Jenny, and he'd certainly experienced it in L.A.

He headed for his father's cubicle, not knowing what to expect.

Zack walked into the glass enclosure and stopped short. Silas's eyes were closed and his complexion was ashen, almost as gray as the hair fringing his head. His mustache was still black but streaked with gray, too. His father was a strapping man—six foot tall and husky. He'd gained weight over the past ten years. Seeing him like this, lying in a bed in a hospital gown, hooked up to IVs and God knew what else, Zack had to absorb the fact his father was aging.

What had Zack thought? That the years would keep passing and his father would remain the same?

His dad's eyes fluttered open, and he stared at Zack for a few seconds without speaking. Finally he said hoarsely, "You came."

Still struck by his father's appearance, Zack didn't respond.

"You didn't want to come, did you?" Silas asked, sounding more like his old self. "This is a duty call."

Was that true? Not entirely, but he didn't admit it. "You had a heart attack," he said without answering the question.

Silas gave a slight shrug. "That's what Jenny tells me. The doc uses words that don't make any sense, and tomorrow, well, I don't know what's going to happen. There's always a chance—"

Zack stepped closer to the bed. "No, there isn't. You're going to have what's called a cardiac catheterization. It's going to show what's wrong and your doctor is going to fix it."

"Sometimes you can find out what's wrong and *not* be able to fix it."

"You can't think that way going into it."

"And here I thought you'd like it if I just faded away and you didn't have to deal with me anymore."

"Don't be ridiculous." Zack said the words, but he *did* feel guilty. Hadn't he often wondered what life would be like without his father's carping?

"Don't lie to me. The truth is the truth is the truth."

No matter what had happened before, Zack said with certainty, "I want you to be well. I want you to be healthy again. Jenny is worried sick about you and she needs you."

His father swallowed, looked away for a moment, then back at him. "She's the daughter I never had. Her own father's a fool for not realizing what a gem he has in her."

Silent, Zack considered Jenny's background and the year he'd been closer to her than he'd ever been to anyone.

Silas asked, "What are you thinking about?"

After a few moments' reluctance, he answered, "How much Jenny meant to Mom and you." And how she'd refused to go with him to L.A. That thought still had the power to bring back bitterness and regret.

"I need you to promise me something," his father entreated in a low, serious voice.

"What?" Zack asked warily.

"With me out of commission, Jenny can't handle the burden of the Rocky D on her own. She's taken over even more responsibility the past couple of months with management of the ranch as well as training the horses, but it's all too big for any one person. So no matter what happens tomorrow, will you stay a month, six weeks, and help her get a handle on whatever has to be done?"

"Dad—"

"I know it's a lot to ask. I know this isn't your life. You have big fish to fry. Well, the Rocky D has big fish, too. I know you think I have no right to ask anything of you. That might be true. But Jenny's going to need some help, and you're the only one I trust to give her that help."

If his father had asked for his own benefit, Zack might have been able to turn him down. But the way he'd put it, how could Zack refuse? Still, he had commitments of his own.

Silas continued, "You could set up shop at the Rocky D for a while. There's plenty of room. You could have your own office in the east wing." He hesitated. "I have a home theater there now, too."

The sliding glass doors of Silas's cubicle opened and a nurse bustled in. "Time's about up," she said gently but firmly. "Your father needs his rest."

Zack knew that was true. He also knew state of mind could make a big difference if his father was to recover. No, he didn't want to stay. No, he didn't want to get roped back into a life he'd left behind. No, he didn't want to be around Jenny and feel that old tug of desire they'd shared.

"Think about it," his father said.

Zack knew he wouldn't be able to do much else.

The following morning, Jenny paced the waiting room while Zack worked on his laptop. She didn't know how he could concentrate with his dad undergoing the heart catheterization. Even during the night as she'd tried to doze on the sofa, she'd caught glimpses of images flickering on the laptop screen where Zack studied them and tapped the computer keys. He hadn't slept at all.

When he'd returned from seeing his dad last night, he'd been remote and silent. This morning, after visiting Silas again, he'd been the same. Just what was going through his head? Once, so many years ago, she would have known. For the past fifteen years, she hadn't had a clue. For the gazillionth time, she thought about what might have been if she hadn't lost their baby. Quickly she shut down those thoughts.

With a long, blown-out breath, Zack closed the lid of the machine, pushed it deeper onto the side table, stood and rolled his shoulders. His muscles rippled under his black T-shirt. Above the waistband of his khakis, she could glimpse just how flat his stomach still was.

"Do you do that often?" she asked, feeling wrinkled and rumpled and not as put together as he had always looked no matter what he wore. The lines around Zack's eyes were deeper now, but other than that he looked… as charismatic and sexy as ever.

"Work through the night? Oh, yeah. Especially when we're on deadline."

"For a movie?"

"For a movie, for an edit, for a casting." He shrugged. "It's the nature of the business."

"Here I thought you lounged in a chaise at the beach most of the time," she joked.

He gave her a long considering look. His blue eyes were so direct with an intense focus that hadn't changed. "My life isn't what it seems from the outside."

"The outside?" She was genuinely curious.

"What you see and hear. The premieres, the publicity for the movies. It looks as if it isn't staged, but all of it is."

"Even those photos of you on the beach?" She wouldn't mention the drop-dead gorgeous models and actresses he was always photographed with.

"Exactly."

Pausing only a second, she prodded, "Does Silas know about your real life, or do you only tell him about the outside?"

"Dad hears what he wants to hear."

"But do you talk about your actual work with him?"

"You probably know how much we talk. It's mostly about the weather, his horse buyers, if I'll be nominated for another Oscar."

"If you made a point of telling him…"

Zack scowled and even that expression was sexy as the corners of his mouth turned down. "You're not going to be on my back about talking to Dad the whole time I'm here, are you? Because if you are, I'm going to spend most of my time working."

If he'd intended to frame that bomb of information into his response, she didn't know. But she surely realized the implication. "The time you're here? How long will that be?"

"We'll figure it out after he's back up here giving orders again."

"We're talking about more than a few days?"

"It depends on his condition. I'll let you know after I speak with his doctor."

For just a moment, Jenny felt her heart fall. She really didn't have a right to be here, or to any information. No matter she spent every day with Silas, saw his symptoms develop, and cared deeply that they had. She wasn't a relative. Zack was his son. She was not Silas's daughter.

That thought brought to mind the inevitable one of wondering where her own father was right now. Maybe she cared so much about Silas because her own dad didn't seem to want her to care about *him*. And she shouldn't, because he always left...he never stayed. But she did care.

"What are you thinking?" Zack asked, as he crossed to the sofa where she sat. He moved the magazine she had tried to concentrate on, lowered himself beside her, yet not too close.

Did he feel any remnant of the attraction that had rippled between them as teenagers? The attraction she felt now? "I'm not thinking. I'm just worried."

"Bull. Something was ticking through that pretty head of yours besides worry."

His attitude both shook and angered her. "You don't

know me anymore, so don't try to read me like a mentalist at a carnival."

"So you think I don't know you?" His voice was lower as he said, "When you're thinking, little frown lines appear right here."

He touched the space between her brows and her heart rapped against her ribs.

"But when you're worrying—" he slid his finger across the side of her mouth "—this dimple disappears and sometimes your lower lip quivers."

She was mesmerized by the pad of his finger on her skin...trembling from skimming her gaze over the breadth of his shoulders, his beard stubble, the past memories in his eyes.

Grabbing her composure for all she was worth, she straightened her shoulders and leaned back. "You're making that up."

"Nope. You haven't changed all that much. You grew up fast and were always direct, curious and sassy. Give me one way you're different now than when you came to live at the Rocky D when you were seventeen."

Instead of an off-the-cuff flip reply, she considered his request. "Now I think before I speak. I hope I've learned to have as much patience with people as I've always had with horses."

He smiled and she wished he hadn't. Zack smiling was almost impossible to resist.

"You think before you speak and have patience with everyone but *me*."

She was about to protest, to tell him he was all wrong, but she considered what he'd said. "I guess with you, my good intentions get short-circuited."

His smile faded. "So tell me what you were thinking."

Zack had always been determined. Maybe this time she shouldn't fight his desire to know. "I was thinking I have no official right to be here...to know Silas's condition. But I'd like to be included."

The cold detachment she'd sensed in Zack when he'd arrived, dissipated altogether. "Of course you'll be included. Has anyone told you differently?"

"Oh, no. The staff and doctors have been understanding."

Zack was studying her as if he knew old insecurities still haunted her. She couldn't let him see that sometimes they did. Most of all, she couldn't let him see that she was still attracted to him.

Rising to her feet, she said, "I'm going to get coffee. I'll bring you a cup."

"Black," he told her as he rose, too, and returned to the laptop.

He'd always taken his coffee black, but she wouldn't let him see she remembered that...along with everything else.

Chapter Two

When Jenny returned to the waiting room with two cups of coffee, Zack wasn't there. She didn't know what to think. Had there been news about Silas? She set down the coffee, noticed Zack's laptop wasn't on the table and was about to ask for information at the nurses' desk when he strode into the waiting room, cell phone in his hand.

"Is Silas finished?" she asked.

"Not that I know of. I locked my laptop in the car and went to make a call." When she glanced at his cell phone, he clipped it onto his belt.

"Business?" she asked, not sure why she was asking. Maybe she just wanted to probe a little.

"Actually, no, it wasn't."

"Someone who wondered where you disappeared to?" She knew she shouldn't be inquiring about this.

His life was none of her business, not anymore. Still, she was curious.

Amused, he asked, "You want details?"

"Only if you want to get them off your chest."

He cast her a wry smile. "No, I don't think I do."

She felt the disappointment like a weight. She should have known better. For all she knew, he was dating three different women at once. That was certainly what the tabloids led everyone to believe. One of the most eligible bachelors in L.A. didn't need to be married or even in a relationship because he was having too much fun. Though from what he'd said last night—

He approached her until he stood close enough to touch. "I left L.A. in a rush. I have lots of loose ends that aren't tied up."

Including a relationship with a woman? she wanted to ask, yet didn't. The one thing she'd learned long ago was never to make the same mistake twice. That was how she'd learned to accept disappointment where her dad was concerned. That was how she'd learned to move on, always looking for a new way to solve a problem, a new way to handle a loss. She'd lost Zack once. She wouldn't make the mistake of feeling too much for him again. It really was as simple as that. Practice had taught her well. Now she had to just keep her wits about her and pretend that being this near to him didn't send a tingle of awareness through her body.

Since she couldn't—wouldn't—ask anything personal, she forced a smile and inquired, "Do you really have a house in Malibu, a penthouse in L.A. and a condo in Vail?"

"Now where did *that* come from?" His forehead furrowed but there was a sparkle of curiosity in his eyes.

"I'm just wondering how much of the tabloid stories about you I can believe."

"Well, at least the real estate I have is one thing they got right. Yes, to all of the above."

"And you've been to every continent?" she pushed.

"I have, for either work or pleasure."

"You actually vacationed in Antarctica?"

At that, he let out a chuckle. "Yes, I did. Why are you so amazed?"

"Because I can't imagine why anyone would want to vacation there."

His blue gaze became more probing. "Jenny, don't you want to see the world?"

"Why would I? I'm happy here."

He shook his head as if he couldn't understand that philosophy at all. "Don't you want to know how other people live? What work means to them…what gives their lives meaning?"

"Does your curiosity get satisfied in your travels?"

He considered that. "I don't know. But I always find answers to some unanswered questions I didn't even know were lurking in my mind. That probably doesn't make any sense to you."

She could see he wasn't talking down to her, but really trying to clarify his point of view. "When *I* want an answer, I just work at finding it right here. But then I guess that's why I gentle horses and you make movies."

"The movie-making might change now."

"How? Why?"

Suddenly, Zack's focus shifted from her to the doorway. When she peered around him, she saw Dr. Murphy,

Silas's cardiologist. He looked serious and she couldn't tell from his expression exactly what had happened.

The cardiac surgeon said, "Zack has signed appropriate forms and instructed me you're to be kept up-to-date on everything that concerns his father's condition."

She murmured to Zack, "Thank you."

His gaze briefly met hers and she gained a momentary glimpse of the young man she'd once loved. The next moment his attention focused on the cardiologist as he asked, "Good news or bad?"

Although Zack might be a visionary behind the camera, Jenny realized he was a pragmatist, too.

"A little of both. There has been heart muscle damage, which we suspected from the myocardial infarction. But we inserted two stents and with a change in lifestyle, I think he'll regain his energy and maybe some of the verve he's lost in the past few months. He's a lucky man…lucky this happened when someone was with him and fortunate an ambulance got him here as soon as it did. No one is ever happy about life changes they need to make to continue good health, but your father seems like a practical man. I'm hoping with the two of you to help convince him, he'll see this as a positive life change, not as something he has to dread. I'll have a nutritionist talk to him before he leaves."

"Can I sit in?" Jenny asked. "He has a housekeeper and I'd like to relay any information to her. Maybe we can devise meals that he doesn't think are too boring."

The doctor smiled. "Diet and exercise will be the two main components of his life changes and…" He motioned to Zack. "Zack told me you'd be a big help with that."

"What about a cardiac rehab program?" Zack asked.

"I'll be speaking with your father about that, too. There are a couple of different ways we can handle it. He'll have to choose what's right for him."

"He'll probably want a private nurse and a home gym," Zack muttered.

The doctor didn't look fazed. He just said, "Whatever it takes."

Jenny knew he was right. She would do whatever it took to keep Silas on the road to good health. Seeing how quickly Zack had responded to her call, she was hopeful he would, too, even if it was only so he could get back to his own life.

"How long do you think it will be until he's able to do the things he wants to do again?" she asked.

"We're going to have to see how his recuperation comes along. But if you're asking in general terms, I'd say four to six weeks at least. Maybe longer until the changes he makes take effect."

Jenny saw Zack frown and didn't know what that meant. Would he consider staying in Miners Bluff that long? If so, why? Did he feel she couldn't handle Silas on her own? Or was he simply worried about his father and didn't want to admit it?

"I'm going to keep him in CICU for today. Tomorrow, if all goes well, I'll transition him to an intermediary room. I want to keep an eye on his blood oxygen level. Then we'll decide what happens next."

Zack extended his hand to shake the cardiologist's. "Thank you."

Jenny did the same, saying, "I wish we weren't so far from the hospital."

"Miners Bluff has a superior urgent care center. Don't hesitate to go there or call me if there are any problems." The doctor moved toward the door. There he stopped. To Zack he said, "Your dad is a tough customer. It might take both of you to convince him to do what he needs to do." Then he exited the room, leaving Zack and Jenny alone—each wondering what came next.

Four days later, Jenny stepped through the mahogany French doors to Silas's parlor, surprised to see Zack cleaning out the cupboard behind the wet bar. "What are you doing?"

Zack didn't know if this was going to be a fight or not, but he wouldn't back down from it. He stacked bottles of liquor into a carton. "I'm clearing away temptation. Dad's resting, I hope?"

They'd driven into Flagstaff together to pick him up when he was discharged. Both wanted to hear what the instructions were for after-care. He was supposed to take it easy for the next week. Zack wasn't sure that meant the same thing to his father that it meant to him.

He continued to remove bottles from the cabinet and shove them in the box. "I know he doesn't like staying in one of the guest bedrooms down here, but it's for his own good. I'll stay down here, too, then I can keep an eye on him."

"He can use the intercom system if he needs you."

Zack stared down into the box so long, Jenny finally asked, "Zack?"

"Sorry. I was remembering... This isn't the first time I've done something like this."

She looked puzzled. "What do you mean?"

Did he want to get into this with her? Why not? The past didn't matter anymore. If she didn't know the gritty details, maybe it was time. "Dad drank and gambled for as far back as I can remember, then he'd come home and fight with Mom. When I was around ten, I got this mistaken impression that if I went through the house and got rid of some of the liquor, that might make a difference. So I'd take out a bottle here, a bottle there and I'd dump them behind the barn. I couldn't wipe out the whole cupboard, there would've been hell to pay. But at least I felt I was doing *something*."

He saw the softening in Jenny's brown eyes and he knew what that meant. It was pity. He certainly didn't want her pity, not for the boy he'd been, and certainly not for the man he was now. "That taught me one very important lesson," he added, suddenly realizing exactly why he was telling her this story. "You can't make a difference in someone's life unless they want you to."

She crossed the hunter green and burgundy Persian rug, rounding a suede and leather sofa. "That's not true, Zack. Don't tell me you believe that."

When she stopped in front of the bar, he focused his gaze on her. "Do you think you've made a difference in his life?" He knew Jenny had poured everything she was and everything she could have been into Silas and the Rocky D.

"I *have* made a difference. Because I've become a substitute for you."

This time there was no pity in her eyes but there was something else he couldn't decipher. That bothered him. He used to understand Jenny so well…why she yearned for bonds she could depend on.

Jenny's father had done his duty by her when he'd had to. His love had always been the rodeo. Early on,

Jenny had had her mom, but had only seen her dad when he came in from the circuit. After that...

Jenny's mom had suddenly died of a brain aneurysm when Jenny was eight and her father had been devastated. Jenny had known, even though he wasn't at home that much, that he and her mom had really loved each other. After a year of Jenny taking care of Charlie, rather than Charlie taking care of *her,* he'd left her with a neighbor more and more, always chasing a rodeo purse and a dream. That's the way it had been until Jenny had done an internship on the Rocky D the summer before her senior year in high school. She'd loved horses, handled them expertly and calmed them, showing up his father's best grooms. His mother had started giving her other responsibilities and had let her handle some of the bookwork. When his mom learned her history, she'd asked Jenny if she wanted to live with them her senior year of high school. Charlie had easily agreed, handing off some of the responsibility for his almost-grown child. Jenny became like a daughter to the Deckers.

Zack's attraction to Jenny and hers to him had revved up the moment she'd set foot on the Rocky D. Zack had known it wouldn't be fair to start something with her, when he intended to leave Miners Bluff as soon as he could. Jenny, on the other hand, wore her heart on her sleeve, which had made it easy for him to confide in her, go on long walks and rides, become close to her in a way he'd never been close to a girl before. The night of their high school graduation, they'd gone to the all-night party, come home around 3:00 a.m. and climbed up to the hayloft, which had become their private place. They'd been so excited. He'd won the National Young

Filmmakers Scholarship and his dad had hired her to be one of his horse trainers and handlers. In that excitement, their threshold of restraint had fallen low. They'd made love in that hayloft. He'd asked her to go with him to L.A. She'd refused. That had been the end of them.

"You didn't have to be a substitute for anyone," Zack protested, feeling as if she were blaming him for something about her life, too.

"I didn't say I didn't want to be here, because I *did*. But I also realized that after your mother died, Silas gave up on the idea that you'd ever come back."

Staying in this house again, recollections from that difficult time in Zack's life pummeled him. As he'd tried to do since he'd returned, he shoved them away. "Even if Mom hadn't died, I doubt if I would have come back. When she visited me in L.A., she made sure to tell me she was proud—of me, of my work... But have you forgotten that when I left for film school, my father cut me off? He didn't want to know how the classes were, or what kind of projects I was doing. He didn't want to know if I was successful. He just didn't care. He'd planned for me to take his place someday. He blamed her for my absence because she gave me my first video camera."

Jenny leaned closer, the bar still a barrier between them. "You're both carrying too many shadows from the past. It's time to let go of all of it."

Just a whiff of Jenny's perfume unsettled Zack and lit fires he'd rather douse. "What about *your* dad, Jenny? Have *you* let go of all of it?" He saw immediately that he'd struck home and he shouldn't have. He shook his head. "I had no right to ask that."

With a sigh, she leaned away. "Maybe you did. After all, I'm giving *you* advice."

With a shrug, he admitted, "I have no advice, not about fathers and their kids." Closing the top of the carton, he taped it then started filling another.

Finally she said, "I've learned something over the years, Zack. I do have to accept reality. Wishing my dad would change only brought me heartache, so I accept him for who he is and don't expect anything. That way I don't get hurt."

Her acceptance of her own father's shortcomings made him feel like a jerk. He shouldn't have complained about the childhood he'd had when Jenny's had been so much worse. Losing her mom as a kid couldn't have been easy. Staying with a neighbor who really wasn't interested in babysitting while her father was gone had to have made Jenny feel unwanted.

She proved that as she told him, "After Mom died and I had to stay with Mildred when Dad left for the circuit, I disappeared into the library downtown and learned everything I could about horses...to fill up my life and I guess my heart, too. I didn't have the guts to come to a place like the Rocky D to learn what I needed to know to become a horse trainer, but I went to smaller ranches, asked if I could help with chores and got paid enough to buy clothes for school. I didn't care about the money as much as I just wanted to be around the animals, to know more about them. Some of those horses were my best friends until I went to high school and really got to know Mikala and Celeste. Up until then I shied away from the other girls because I felt they made fun of me...and looked down on me. Celeste and I had a lot in common because we were both girls from the wrong side of the tracks. I'm not sure how Mikala hooked up with us, maybe because her mother wasn't around much when she was growing up. But they became my safety net—they were always there for me. How did you and Dawson and Clay become friends?"

"The reverse of you and Celeste and Mikala, I guess. Our families went back to the founding fathers of Miners Bluff. In one way or another, we were all rebelling against authority, against our fathers, our families. Don't get me wrong, we didn't talk about it. Guys didn't do that." He shot her a wry grin. "But we knew we all wanted to be independent and forge our own course, no matter what anybody else thought."

"Rebels *with* a cause?" she joked.

"Minus the motorcycles. Clay and I used horses. Dawson had a Mustang."

She laughed at the pun.

Whenever he and Jenny found a nonvolatile subject, he enjoyed the ease of talking to her, just as he had when he was a teenager.

In high school, they'd all hung out at Mikala's aunt's bed and breakfast where her refrigerator and pantry was overstocked with everyone's favorite drinks and snacks. As he and Jenny started spending more time alone after she moved in at the Rocky D, long talks about anything and everything had taken place in the barn and hayloft. Long talks...and plenty of kisses....

But they weren't kids anymore and the shadow of him leaving and her refusal to go with him sidled in and out between them now, along with the electricity that never seemed to cease buzzing.

"Is there anywhere else you think I should look for a stash like this?" He waved at the remaining bottles.

"You could ask me," Silas said from the doorway. Both Zack and Jenny jumped, startled by his appearance.

"All right," Zack agreed quickly, deciding to face his father head-on in everything now. "Is there anyplace else you'd like me to clean out?" He tried to ignore the fact that his father was leaning on a cane and looking pale. His physician had warned them not to expect too much too soon, but it was hard seeing his father like this.

Silas entered the room and straightened up to his full six-foot height. "You don't have to clean anything out. I haven't had a drop of liquor for a year. I keep that assortment for my friends, or for cocktail parties, like the one I had to introduce Clay Sullivan to some possible clients. It was the same night we all watched your new movie."

That derailed Zack's thoughts. "You got a pirated copy?"

"I did. I didn't want to wait for the premiere."

Sometimes Zack forgot how well his father was connected. "You never told me you watched it."

"Does it matter?"

Good question—and he really wasn't sure of the answer. Did he want to know what his father thought about it? Chances were good Silas would have something critical to say. Not that Zack couldn't take criticism. He'd had to take plenty of it to get where he was now. But coming from his father, it would be nice to hear something positive, some sort of encouragement or pat on the back he'd never gotten as a kid.

Silas stroked his mustache. "If you're looking for cigars in addition to the liquor, you'll find a box in my bottom desk drawer in my office. They're underneath the Bible. I haven't had a smoke in the past six months."

As Zack looked into his father's eyes, he wished he could believe him. But after years of hearing his dad lie to his mother so many times, he knew trust hadn't even been a word in his father's vocabulary.

Deciding to leave this discussion for the present, Zack asked his dad, "Is there anything I can bring you from upstairs to make you more comfortable down here?"

"I'll only be comfortable when I'm in my own room again," Silas grumbled.

Jenny, who'd been absorbing the conversation, stepped in. "It's only for a few days, Silas. Besides, you'll have a great view of the back pasture from the guest room. You can watch the yearlings when we let them out on the nice days."

"Nice days?" Silas barked. "You won't be seeing many more of them. I heard we're in for snow next week."

"So you can watch them frolic in the snow when I exercise them," she responded, unfazed.

"While I eat sawdust and vegetables."

"Do you think I'd let Martha serve you sawdust and vegetables? I'm smarter than that. We're going to make such tasty recipes you won't be able to resist."

Finally, Silas broke into a slow smile. "If anybody can do it, you can." He sighed and ran a hand through his halo of gray hair. "Already I'm more tired than if I'd ridden out to Feather Peak. Jeez, how long is this going to last?"

"You know what the doctor said. It could be a while—a month, two, maybe even three. But with a new diet and some exercise when you're ready, you'll be feeling better soon, Silas. I promise you."

He looked at her the way a doting father looks at a loving daughter. "Your promises I believe."

With a last glance at Zack, he said, "I'll make that list."

After Silas had gone, his cane tapping on the hardwood floor down the hall, Zack turned to Jenny, feeling somewhat unnerved by witnessing the bond that had developed between her and his dad. Was he envious of it? Yet how could he be when it had been *his* choice to put his dad in the recesses of his life for so many years?

"What if he doesn't feel better in three months?" he challenged her. "What if the way he's feeling now is as good as it gets? That happens, you know."

"Maybe so. But I can't think that way and Silas doesn't need *you* thinking that way. We have to encourage him, day by day." She studied Zack for so long it made him uncomfortable.

"What?"

"I don't think you're used to encouraging *anyone*, are you?"

"That's not true. I deal with temperamental actors all the time."

"That isn't the same thing at all. I'm talking about common kindness, compassion and an optimistic attitude to make someone *want* to get better, want to do their best in life, not in a make-believe world."

"Do you think I deal with make-believe? Have you even *watched* any of my movies?"

That made Jenny's cheeks flush. "Of course I have. I'm sorry. That didn't come out right. I know you don't just produce and direct entertainment. There's always more than that to it, a bigger cause, an issue under the surface."

So she'd realized that about him, had she? He didn't know whether he'd expected her to be perceptive about his motives or not. "That's one reason why I'm moving into documentaries. I don't want to hide the cause anymore. I want to go after it. I have the clout and the money to do that now. I can film the stories I want to film."

"Did you ever think about what you'd be doing if you hadn't won that award in high school? Where you'd be now?"

He couldn't tell if she was really asking about *them* or his life in general. Anytime they got near the personal, the vibrations between them picked up, the attraction he still felt for her ignited. "I still would have found a way to get to L.A. with or without my dad's approval, with or without his money. You know that. It was that important for me to get away from here and find a life of my own."

"And what if your career hadn't worked out so well? What if success hadn't come easy?"

"Easy? Is that really what you think?"

Moving around the bar, she helped him pull bottles from the cupboard. "It seemed like it. You went to film school, then you were directing your first movie which was a hit. Then you directed another and then another."

When Zack reached into the cupboard, his shoulder grazed hers and a jolt of awareness hit him in the gut. He leaned away before she could see how that minor contact rocked him.

Clearing his throat, he said, "It did seem like that from the outside, didn't it? That first film was a technical success, but not an industry success. For a year I worked in the stables outside of Anaheim to make money to keep a one-room apartment. I was still sending out résumés, reading scripts, thinking about what to do to make a career work. I directed a rock video that caught notice and put me in touch with the right people. One of them hired me as an assistant director. After that, I worked day and night, took any project I thought would get some notice until finally, I got my chance. A director backed out and I was in. *That* movie was an industry success. That movie won me my first Oscar."

"I never knew you had to work so hard. Did Silas know?"

"Are you kidding? When I left, he told me he knew I'd come running back with my tail between my legs. There was no way in hell I wasn't going to make my life out there work."

And he'd been willing to make the two of them work, too. If only Jenny had come with him. If only she had tried, maybe then he wouldn't still feel resentment and bitterness along with an attraction that wouldn't fade. The sooner he was back in L.A. again, the better. But he'd made his father a promise, to stay here long enough so Jenny wouldn't have the burden of running the Rocky D all on her own. He regretted that promise now. Looking into Jenny's soft brown eyes, feeling his body respond to her, he knew his stay was going to be nothing but torture—on many fronts.

"What's wrong?" she asked softly. "You look… angry."

"You don't want to know."

"I wouldn't have asked if I didn't want to know."

He was quiet for a moment. "Did you ever imagine what your life might have been like if you had come with me?"

She looked surprised, as if she'd never expected that question to pop up. "I...I never wanted that kind of life."

"How did you know when you hadn't tried it?" Then he lifted his hand in a dismissive gesture. "Never mind. I shouldn't have asked. During those couple of tough years, you wouldn't have stuck by me. I know what you went through with your dad. You would have thought it was just more of the same."

She looked as if he'd slapped her. There was real hurt in her eyes. He'd never meant to cause that. Or had he? Did he want her to feel the same pain he'd felt when she said she couldn't go with him? This was so ridiculous, revisiting history that couldn't be rewritten.

He shook his head. "I shouldn't have brought it up. We made the decisions we did."

In a quiet voice, she asked, "Where has your heart gone, Zack? You talk as if you have nothing but your work. Is that the way it is?"

"Work is everything, isn't it, Jenny? Isn't that why you stay here? What else do *you* have?"

She was quick to answer. "I have Silas. I also have friends and a sense of belonging in Miners Bluff. I have a life here, Zack. All of that is more important to me than just work."

Zack's cell phone buzzed and he was actually relieved for the interruption. Taking it from his belt, he checked the caller ID. "Speaking of friends, it's Dawson. He's returning my call. I'd better take this."

Jenny studied him as if she hadn't expected him to stay in touch with old friends.

He explained quickly, "Dawson, Clay and I kept in touch over the years. Dawson flies out for Lakers games now and then. Clay sends me photos and video clips of Abby. I can't believe she's growing as fast as she is."

He opened his cell and would have passed Jenny without a glance, but she caught his arm, saying, "You stay. I'll go." The impression of her fingers burned through his sweater. The room felt hot and he knew it was definitely time to put distance between the two of them.

She hesitated as if she wanted to say so much more, but clearly thought better of it as she released his arm. "I'll see how Silas is making out with that list."

Zack wished she would take his memories and regrets with her.

"Hey, Dawson," Zack said, watching Jenny leave the room. The scent of jasmine that always seemed to surround her still lingered in the air.

"Sorry for the phone tag," Dawson apologized. "Construction's picking up again and we're swamped."

"How's Luke?"

There was a long hesitation on Dawson's part, as if he didn't talk about his son easily these days. It had been over a year and a half since Dawson's wife died and Zack knew the boy was having problems getting over his mom's death. Dawson had talked to him about it when Luke's school grades had tanked, when he'd started getting in trouble, when Dawson was at his wit's end because counselors hadn't seemed able to help.

"That's why I'm calling, Zack. Come January and the start of a new school term, I'm going to move us back to Miners Bluff."

"You're kidding."

"No, I'm not. I've been considering it ever since I spoke to Mikala Conti at the reunion. You know she's a music therapist."

"I knew she was a counselor. I just didn't realize what her specialty was."

"Luke is into music. He spends more time with the piano and his iPod than with schoolwork or with me. When I mentioned that to Mikala, she said it could be a starting point. I'm willing to give anything a shot. Nothing here is helping."

Zack knew Dawson's life in Phoenix was high stress, long hours, with lots of monetary rewards. He had a huge house in Fountain Hills and more money than he'd ever need. But money wasn't doing his son any good.

"Luke needs a supportive community around him," Dawson continued. "And Mikala has a high success rate, according to the psychologist who has been treating Luke here. If Mikala could just get him started turning around so that he and I could at least communicate, that would mean everything."

"What about the business?"

"I can handle it lots of ways. Dad's a great manager when it comes to my crews. I can run everything long distance, at least temporarily. I have to try this, Zack, because I don't know what else to do. It's the first time in my life I've felt powerless. I hate it."

Dawson was the CEO of his own construction company. He handled workers, payrolls, new design projects, architects. Zack had an idea of his frustration now.

"I'm back in Miners Bluff for the moment," he revealed to his friend.

"You're kidding! You've been away for years, now suddenly two visits in a few months? What happened?"

"Dad had a heart attack."

"Zack, I'm sorry. How is he?"

"He just came home today. I'm going to be here for the next few weeks, so if there's anything you need to know before you make the move, just give me a call."

"Do you have work to keep you busy while you're there?"

"Some. There's a new project I'm thinking about doing. I can do a lot of the research from here."

"Give your dad my regards."

"I'll do that. And you call me if you need anything."

"I will. I'll be driving up there some time after the first of the year to look at the school. If you're still there—"

"No way will I still be here."

Dawson chuckled. "Try not to go stir crazy. I'll give you a call in a couple of weeks to see how your dad is."

"Thanks, Dawson. I'll talk to you soon."

Zack closed his phone and clipped it onto his belt, wishing he could do something concrete to help his friend. He couldn't imagine having a child and watching him suffer.

He hadn't thought much about being a father...until now. He didn't date women who had motherhood on their minds. Maybe he should think about dating a different type of woman. A woman like...

Jenny?

No, he told himself. They were over.

Chapter Three

Golden sunrise drifted over the pastures of the Rocky D, defying the colder weather that had moved in since the beginning of November. Jenny loved early mornings this time of year, when one season teetered on the brink of another. This early, Silas's three permanent hands, Hank, Tate and Ben, were already at work. The horses weren't yet restless to be let out, to be let free. She could forget about what problems the day might bring with Zack and Silas under the same roof and have some time for herself.

She led Songbird from her stall, rubbed her nose and asked conversationally, "Ready for a rough and tumble ride?"

"And just what *is* a rough and tumble ride?" a deep male voice asked from behind.

Jenny turned and saw Zack coming down the walkway. "You're up early," she said lightly, ignoring her racing heart.

"I usually am. I thought I'd go for a ride instead of doing an early-morning workout. Mind if I join you?"

Had anyone told Zack she rode every morning? Had he come out here purposely to talk to her about something? He seemed to be waiting for an answer so she responded, "I don't mind. Which horse would you like?"

"Tattoo."

He'd already picked one out? "How do you know you're compatible?"

He laughed. "Only *you* would ask something like that. I was down here last night. Tattoo and I struck up a conversation and we're well along to becoming friends. So...any problem with me taking him out?"

"No." She hesitated, then asked, "Why did you come down here last night?" When he gave her a studying look, she said, "Sorry, none of my business, I guess."

"It was after dinner. You were discussing new recipes with Martha. Dad was on the phone with Clay's father. I thought I'd take a look around. Everything's been kept up well. I noticed the mares' barn had a new roof."

"Last year."

"Are you still attracting clients from across the country who want cutting horses for competitions?"

"Yes."

"And the boarders' barn is full."

"Always."

Zack had to pass her to reach Tattoo's stall. He was dressed in jeans, boots and a sheepskin jacket this morning.

"You couldn't have brought that along," she said gesturing to his coat.

"Nope. It was hanging in the closet in my old room. I'd forgotten about it. It was huge when Mom bought it for me. Now it fits."

Jenny could almost see the memories in Zack's eyes, some bittersweet, some warm and some painful. She wasn't sure what to say.

"We can talk about her, Jen. All my memories of her have been limited to the photographs I took along and the videos I made. I have never had anyone to talk to about her. Do you know what I mean?"

"I do. I mean I talk to Dad about Mom when he's around, which isn't often, but I don't really have anything of hers except the funny hat she used to wear to church. I took it from the bag Dad was giving to Goodwill after she died. I know things are just things, but they seem to mean a lot after someone's gone. The pearl earrings your mom gave me for high school graduation are one of my prized possessions."

"You wore them the night of the reunion."

"You noticed?"

The quiet of the stables seemed to breed intimacy, and this morning was no different. This was the everyday barn, where favorite horses were lodged, where personal tack was kept, where the hayloft up above whispered about the kisses shared there when she and Zack were teenagers. And not only kisses. On that graduation night—

"I noticed," he responded, and she didn't know now if they were talking about earrings or so much more. This was dangerous territory for both of them. Especially for her. Since his return, her secret seemed to be on the tip of her tongue, ready to spill out. But there was no reason to tell him about her pregnancy and miscarriage... no reason to hurt him with something they couldn't change. With him standing there, looking down at her, all brawny and handsome in the sheepskin jacket and jeans, she knew she needed some cool air to capture her equilibrium once again.

"Let's saddle up," she suggested a bit shakily.

Zack just gave her an imperceptible nod and moved away.

Ten minutes later they were on the trail. This time of year, the most impressive aspect of the landscape was the mountains in the distance—Moonshadow Mountain and beyond it, Feather Peak.

"Have you ridden to Horsethief Canyon lately?" Zack asked.

Horsethief Canyon led up to Feather Peak. She and Zack had spent time there as teenagers, exploring, hiking, making out.

"No, not lately. Celeste and Clay have. They spent a honeymoon weekend there."

"You were at their wedding?"

"*In* their wedding. It was beautiful. They exchanged vows in Clay's backyard even though his parents probably would have preferred something more elaborate."

"Clay was always good at standing up to his dad."

"I think he and Mr. Sullivan have come to a new understanding since he and Celeste married."

They rode along the fence line until it gave way to rockier terrain. Both horses snorted as if begging to be let loose. Jenny felt the same way. Riding side by side with Zack, she felt edgy, awkward, unlike herself.

"So how about that rough and tumble ride?" he asked with a grin that could always make her breath hitch.

She tossed him a smile over her shoulder and then took off.

She heard Tattoo's hooves behind her steadily, easily keeping up, not trying to overtake her. She thought this might become a race, but Zack wasn't racing. When she cast a glance back at him, he looked intense as he usually did, but also as if he was having a good time.

The morning cold reddened her cheeks, numbed her nose, cooled her breath, but she loved every exhilarating moment of it. Zack galloped past her at one point and she strove to overtake him again, but she couldn't. He didn't just keep riding ahead, however. At a grove of pines he reined in his horse and waited for her. She knew this stand of trees quite well. She and Zack had sought their shade and cool comfort that final spring, when everything just seemed to be beginning. His face was ruddy, too, now from the cold, his hair windblown, his sheepskin collar turned up against the breeze.

"This is magnificent country," he said, almost to himself.

"I can't imagine anywhere as beautiful as this." The sky was already topaz-blue, devoid of clouds, hovering protectively over the landscape.

"Do you want to dismount for a few minutes? The trees will provide a buffer against the wind."

Something about being on the ground within the barrier of trees where they'd once spent time seemed dangerous to Jenny. Yet she wasn't going to be a coward about this. She'd just be very careful.

Zack tethered his horse to a low-slung branch and waited as she did the same. Then in the golden morning light, he found the old path covered with pine needles and dried leaves from the aspen in the not-too-far distance. There was a hushed quality within the grove that Jenny had always liked, that gave her a sense of peace.

Zack followed the path until they were deep inside the grove where sunlight and shadows dappled the ground.

"Soon this could be covered in snow," she reminded him. "If we've had a snowfall, sometimes after the kids finish their lessons, we come out here and play. They bring their saucers and tubes, and it's great fun."

"What kids?" he asked with a curious look.

"I give riding lessons. I do it on a sliding scale and take a few pro-bono students who can't afford to pay. They learn how to ride and groom, and just forget anything that's troubling them."

"Like you did."

"Horses have many lessons to teach, but I give these children goals and they have a sense of accomplishment when they learn how to master riding. I'm hoping those skills will stay with them well into the future."

Zack was standing beside a tall fir. She went still when she recognized it.

"What is it?" Zack asked, following her gaze. Then he saw the bark of the tree. Their names were carved there, deeply enough to have lasted all these years.

"I can't believe the weather hasn't worn them away."

"Or a lightning strike," Zack said nonchalantly. But she knew he was remembering the day he carved them there. They'd had exams at school that week and had come riding out here one day to let off steam, to forget about studying, to be together. She'd been so innocent. He'd been so noble. They'd kissed and made out, and she'd known he wanted her. Yet more than once, he'd insisted it wouldn't be fair if they became really intimate because he'd be leaving.

"You carved our names there, so there would be something lasting of our friendship." They would have had so much more that was lasting if she hadn't had the miscarriage. Yet what would they have done? Even if she had told Zack, would she have joined him in California and regretted it?

"Not much is lasting, is it?" he asked rhetorically.

"Friendships last. We both have proof of that."

"Maybe our high school friendships are the ones that matter most. I don't have friends in L.A. like Clay and Dawson. Even though we don't see each other often, we can pick up wherever we left off."

"Are you *sure* you don't miss Miners Bluff?"

He didn't answer right away, just studied their names, the tall firs, the land that he'd roamed when he was younger. "You can miss something but not need it or count on it or want it in your life anymore."

She wondered if he was feeding himself a line, or if he really believed that. "I think you don't want to admit you miss it. I think you don't want to admit you miss your father."

"Miss the arguments and his disagreeable view of my life?"

"He's proud of you."

"Maybe you've heard that, but I haven't. When I scored the most points in a basketball game, he was proud of me. When I gentled a horse he couldn't get near, he was proud of me. But when I picked up a camera, when I attempted to give him a look at the visions

I wanted to create, he turned the other way. A kid can only take so much of that."

"But you're not a kid anymore."

Zack's gaze became set and somber. "No, I know what I want. I detached from Dad and what he thinks of me." As if he'd grown tired of being on the defensive, he motioned to the land beyond the tree growth. "And what about you, Jenny? Just why did you stay? Out of loyalty, or out of a chance that all this could be yours someday?"

There was something in his voice that disconcerted her. Suspicion? "What do you mean?"

He only hesitated a moment before he said, "I left. I wasn't coming back. The longer you stayed, the more entrenched you became. You loved my mother and she loved you. But after she died, then why did you stay?"

"Because Silas needed me. Because by then the Rocky D was part of *me,* too."

He studied her as if he was looking at a scene he didn't quite know how to edit. "Tell me something, Jenny. Are you included in Dad's will?"

She was absolutely shocked by the direction of his thoughts. Did he believe that she'd hung on to a job here because it would pay off someday? That with him gone, she'd seen an opportunity and she'd taken it? That after his mother died, she could somehow convince his father *she* was the heir?

Insulted beyond measure, she couldn't even speak. Had her refusal to go with him caused this cynicism? Had his sense of betrayal grown into something insidious that made him think of her as an opportunist?

Without a word, she spun around and headed for her

horse. She'd already untethered him when she heard Zack call, "Jenny."

Ignoring the sound of her name on his lips, ignoring the voice that could always affect her so deeply, she mounted Songbird, clicked her tongue and took off for the Rocky D. The boy Zack had once been had been taken over by a man she absolutely didn't know.

The crunch of tires on gravel from cars and trucks pulling into the space between the everyday barn and the mares' barn on Saturday morning pulled Zack from his office where he sat listening by the intercom in case his father needed him. As if that would happen. Silas wasn't asking for a thing from him, not even a glass of water. He was relying on Jenny and Martha.

The door to his father's room was slightly open. Zack peered in and found Silas working on a crossword puzzle. "Dad, I'm going out to the barn." Zack lifted his cell phone. "You have my number on speed dial, right?"

"Filling out a crossword puzzle isn't too strenuous for me," his father muttered, waving him away. "I'll be fine."

Leaving his work behind, Zack headed for the kitchen door. Martha was already sautéing something for lunch.

"Smells good," he said with a smile for her.

"Jenny and I concocted this recipe. We'll see if your dad's ready to become part vegetarian." Martha had brown hair with blond highlights and was in her late forties. She'd been the Rocky D's chief cook and housekeeper since Zack's teenage years. Her quarters were behind the kitchen and like everyone else on the Rocky D, she was more like family than an employee.

"If you can win him over to vegetables, you deserve a raise."

She gave him a quick grin as she shuffled the vegetables in the pan.

As if his sixth sense about Jenny was still functioning, Zack spotted her outside the barn talking to a group of kids. She'd just pointed them toward the arena when she stepped aside to have a conversation with a woman who looked to be about her own age.

He knew he should apologize to Jenny, but whenever he thought about it, he realized that wouldn't be quite honest. He'd voiced some of the thoughts that had niggled at him for all these years. Why had she stayed? Because his mother had become the role model she'd missed? Because Silas was a substitute father? Or because she'd seen the opportunity to become part of a family that in the end could benefit her in so many ways?

When Jenny had refused to go with him, he'd thought about all of this. The longer he'd been in L.A., he'd thought about it even more. From his own experience, he'd learned women often wanted to latch on to him because of what he had to offer, not because of who he was. In fact, he'd broken off a relationship before the reunion. He'd learned a woman he'd been dating for a couple of months had used his name as a reference when she'd gone to a bank to apply for a small business loan. Rachel Crandall had never mentioned a loan to him, never asked him if it would be okay to use his name. Afterward, when he'd told her he was going out of the country soon and didn't feel their relationship was going to work, she'd arrived at his penthouse, all perfumed and tempting, her dress so tight he didn't know how she'd gotten into it. She'd pouted, she'd pleaded and finally she'd come right out and asked him for money. He'd known then their matchup had been all about money for her, or at least what she could get.

He'd again nixed the idea of any investment in her on his part and she'd left in a huff. As soon as the door had closed, he'd known he wasn't going to miss her.

On the other hand, while he'd been in England, he hadn't been able to stop thinking about how beautiful Jenny had looked at the reunion in her yellow dress, or how she'd looked in jeans with a bandanna around her neck and a straw hat on her head fifteen years before.

Approaching the women at the barn, he froze when he heard the brunette say, "Stan doesn't want me to bring the kids for lessons. He insists he won't take handouts. I just don't understand the man anymore. We're behind on our utilities and the rent. I can see Michael and Tanya are worrying about us. They hear us arguing about money, talking about where we might go if we have to leave the house, and I just want to give them some happiness. They love your lessons. I want to be on the same page as my husband, but with this, I can't be. We're not going to have money for Christmas gifts this year and this is the least I can do for them, thanks to you."

Jenny reassured her. "Helen, if your husband calls me, I'll do my best to convince him to let Michael and Tanya keep coming."

Helen gave Jenny a wan smile. "Thank you."

"Is there anything else I can do for you?" Jenny asked her. "You know the community will be delivering food baskets for the holidays. I can put your name on the list."

"Stan would never accept a food basket. He went into

Flagstaff today to apply for a job at an electrical company. Say a few prayers for us that it comes through."

"I will," Jenny said, and Zack knew that she meant it. He waited until Helen went to the car and said over her shoulder, "I'll be back at noon."

Jenny spotted him then. Their gazes met briefly but she turned away, heading toward the arena.

He caught up to her easily. "Tough conversation," he said.

She glanced over at him, but she kept silent.

"You've given me the cold shoulder for forty-eight hours. Is this the way it's going to be?"

This time she stopped, hands on her hips. "I don't know. You tell me. Why would you want to talk to someone with ulterior motives like mine?"

She was angry, but he could tell from the expression in her dark brown eyes, she was hurt, too.

"Damn it. Do something for me," he suggested. "Try to imagine yourself in my shoes. I thought we had something to build on and you refused to take a chance with me. All these years you've stayed here when you're young, beautiful and talented. You could go anywhere and do anything you wanted. So from my perspective, what would *you* think?"

"So you didn't accuse me of being an opportunist because I was backing you into a corner? You really *meant* it? You really *don't* trust me?" She seemed horrified at the thought.

Before he considered how to word his answer, she asked, "Do you trust *anyone?*"

"I trust Clay and Dawson."

"You don't trust your accountant, your lawyer, people

who work for you?" She shook her head. "What kind
of life do you have out there?"

He wasn't sure what he heard in her voice, but he
didn't like it. "I have a life I like—the life I've always
wanted."

She searched his face. Her gaze dropped to his lips.
Then she turned away from him so he couldn't see her
thoughts in her expression and headed for the arena
again. "I've got to get to those kids. Hank can get them
started, but they're a lot to handle."

"How many in the class?"

"It varies."

"Ages?"

"Eight to eleven."

"Mind if I watch?"

"I don't mind as long as you don't get in the way."

He grinned at her. "You won't even know I'm there."

Twenty minutes later Zack's words echoed in Jenny's
head. Oh, she knew he was here all right. In his black
crew neck sweater, jeans and boots he was an imposing presence whether she wanted to admit it or not. At
first, he'd stood at the arena's entrance watching her
and Hank help the children mount, making sure their
helmets were secure. But then he'd come closer, studying what they were doing. Jenny was on her horse leading the class in a circle while Hank was on the ground
watching for any problems. One of the boys' boots kept
slipping out of his stirrups and Hank had gone to help
him adjust them.

However, the next time she looked behind her shoulder, Zack had Helen's son, eleven-year-old Michael, to
one side and was talking to him in a low voice, show-

ing him something with his hands. She didn't want to break the circle and distract the other kids, so she kept giving directions, leading them in a figure eight. Soon, however, Michael joined them and he seemed to have better control of his horse. He was all smiles and she couldn't help but wonder what had taken place between him and Zack.

She'd never seen Zack with kids. What kind of father would he be? What kind of father would he have been? One thing was certain—she was never going to tell him about the miscarriage. She just wasn't. Only Silas and Olivia had known. She hadn't even told Mikala and Celeste. Her pregnancy had been such a scary secret that she'd only confided in Zack's mother. Then when the miscarriage happened, Silas had to know, but that was as far as it had gone. Except, of course, for the doctor Olivia had rushed her to.

Now, crazily, the wave of loss came rushing back. Years had passed. She had to admit when she babysat Clay and Celeste's little girl, Abby, longings tugged at her heart. "What ifs" rushed into her head. She'd had lots of practice with staying in the moment. The problem was, Zack's return had mixed the past with the present.

True to his word, Zack didn't interfere with the class. He just sat on one of the bales of hay, his long legs stretched out in front of him, ankles crossed, as if he didn't have a care in the world. But Jenny sensed more was going on under the surface than he'd ever admit. Returning to the Rocky D had obviously stirred up old feelings and resentment, old bitterness, maybe even a feeling of home he hadn't experienced for a while.

At the end of class, Hank and Jenny helped the kids

with their mounts and their tack, then Zack did, too. When he saw the children were going to groom their horses, he passed out the brushes.

A moment later, he stopped to talk to Michael. Zack said something and Michael laughed and she wondered how the two of them had formed a bond so quickly. Sometimes Michael and his sister had worry written all over them. She was glad to see Zack could help Michael forget some of what was going on at home.

She said easily, "I see the two of you have met."

"Yeah," Michael answered. "Zack taught me how to hold the reins so Firecracker listened. I was having an awful time turning him."

After a glance at Zack, Jenny asked, "What did he tell you?"

"He didn't tell me. He *showed* me. I was confusing Firecracker. Zack said my hands had to be gentle and easy, yet clear. If I wanted him to go right, all I had to do was tug the reins that way and give him a little nudge with my left foot, and it worked. I kept up and didn't get out of line once."

"Well, I'm glad to see you're pleased, but you don't always have to stay in line. And if you need help, all you have to do is ask me."

"I know." His voice lowered. "I don't want to seem stupid to the other kids."

"I don't think any of them would think that, Michael. You catch on quickly. I'm glad you learned gentleness with Firecracker works best."

"Did you know Zack makes movies?" Michael asked her, wide-eyed and in awe.

"Apparently, his dad told him someone famous was staying at the Rocky D right now," Zack interjected. "I guess the whole town knows about Silas's heart attack and why I came home."

"My dad said it was on the news channel," Michael offered helpfully.

Zack grimaced.

"His picture was on there and everything," Michael added. "That's how I knew he was the one my dad was talking about."

"I have a job like most people. Mine just happens to involve shooting film," Zack explained.

Michael looked down at his shoeboots. "I wish my dad had a job, then maybe he wouldn't be so grumpy."

Zack exchanged a look with Jenny. "It's hard for a man not to have the work he likes to do. Work not only pays the bills, but it makes a man or a woman feel like he or she is accomplishing something. What do you want to be when you grow up?"

"I don't know, but I sure do like riding and taking care of horses."

Zack stood again. "I always liked that, too."

"But that's not what your work is," Michael pointed out.

"No, it isn't. I miss being around horses."

"If you're famous and rich, then you could have some," the eleven-year-old said as if life was as easy as that.

Zack laughed. "I suppose I could, but I'm not in one place very long. If I had horses, I'd like to be there to take care of them myself, not let someone else do it."

"My mom says Tanya and I can learn responsibility coming to this class."

"You already are," Jenny insisted. "You're grooming your horse yourself and you take care of your own tack."

"Maybe I could ride my bike out here and help you with chores and I could earn money for Christmas."

Jenny didn't know what to say to that. Finally, she responded, "Instead of earning money to buy things, maybe you could give your mom and dad something they'd enjoy that wouldn't cost anything."

Michael thought about that. "You mean like taking out the garbage without being told?"

"Sure, something like that."

He didn't seem impressed by the idea.

Zack said, "If you think about it, I'm sure you can be creative." Zack held out his hand to Michael and said, "It was good to meet you."

Michael shook his hand, too. "I'll have to tell my dad you're just a regular guy."

Zack smiled. "I'll make the rounds and see if anyone else needs help."

Jenny watched him walk away with a lump in her throat. She told herself again Zack couldn't mean anything to her now. But watching him interact with Michael had made her wonder once more what might have happened if her pregnancy had gone to term. It made her wonder again exactly what kind of father Zack would be.

Chapter Four

On Monday evening, Jenny and Zack drove down Copper Mine Boulevard to the town square. She couldn't help noticing he was moodier than usual, and she was pretty sure of the reason for his demeanor. "You didn't want to sub for your dad at this meeting, did you?"

Straightening in his seat now, his head practically hit the ceiling of the pickup. "Another committee meeting to decide something about Miners Bluff? I *hate* this kind of thing. Besides that, it's not even about something important. This committee is going to decide on the decorations for the gazebo, square and outlying streets. Dad always offered money to back whatever decorations they wanted. He still will, even if he isn't there. So I don't understand why they need my opinion."

Her silence in the cab of the truck seemed to bother him. "Say it."

"Say what?" she innocently asked.

"What's on your mind."

"You should look beneath the surface."

"Of stringing lights on the gazebo?"

"No, of what the season means to your dad...how the part he plays in Miners Bluff contributes to his worth, and I don't mean monetarily. He's tired. He doesn't feel as if he can do anything he used to do—not with any verve—so he's frustrated. If he can't do it, then he wants someone to do it for him."

"Do what?"

"Be there. Have a say. Maybe even give a few ideas that will pretty up the town for Christmas."

Zack rested his hand on his thigh, one very muscular thigh. Jenny remembered the feel of his legs against hers while they'd briefly danced at the reunion. That memory brought back another picture she put away to think about later.

"My dad has always been manipulative. He sees this meeting as a way to get me involved in Miners Bluff."

"Would that be so bad?" Jenny asked.

"It's not bad. It's not good. It's just *not* going to happen. I don't even know if I'll be here 'til Christmas, so why care about the lights and decorations?"

Jenny pulled into a parking slot she found in front of a lawyer's office. Light snow had begun to fall and she knew that wasn't going to help Zack's mood any. He was used to California sun. Yet he didn't complain as they stepped out of the truck.

He checked his watch. "We're early. Let's take a walk in the park before we get cooped up in one of those meeting rooms in the town hall."

"Sure. We can walk to the gazebo."

They ambled across the street to the park that sat at the center of town. Signs detailing the history of Miners Bluff were posted at two of the entrances, and at this hour, walkways through the park were lit by tall, old-fashioned streetlamps that cast a soft glow through bare maple, oak and sycamore branches. The snow floating into the lighted path was absolutely beautiful as it sugared everything it touched.

He suddenly stopped and she could see he was focusing on the here and now and where they were, rather than on where he wanted to be. She had to wonder exactly where that was. His gaze targeted the gazebo that they were heading toward, the benches on the pathways, the white picket fence surrounding the outskirts of the park.

"It hasn't changed," he noted.

"Not much. The gazebo gets a fresh coat of paint every other year. The lamplights have new energy-saving bulbs. But other than that, it's the park of your youth."

"I didn't come into town much as a kid. Everything we needed at the Rocky D was brought to us."

"You never came here to ride those big swings over there? Or climb on the jungle gym?"

"I was always too busy with the horses, or exploring areas of the ranch where Dad particularly didn't want me to go. This park was just a place we came to for special events, holiday celebrations, summer festivals. But it wasn't really part of my life. How about you?"

Jenny was slow to answer because she had to think about what she wanted to say. She could just gloss over the truth, but, after all, this was Zack. "I met my first horse here when I was about five," she said with a smile.

"It was a Shetland pony and it was love at first sight. I remember my mom smoothing her hand over my hair and saying one of these days when Dad won a great big purse, he'd buy me a horse. Someday we'd move out of the trailer and live in a real home."

Jenny shrugged as if it was all really in the past. "But someday never came. I sneaked into the rodeos as often as I could in summers, talked to the owners, got their permission to handle their horses. But from fall to spring when I needed someplace to go, I came here. I know we're talking about hanging Christmas decorations and that doesn't seem important to you. But when I was a kid, I loved to look at the flowers planted around the trees, the ivy growing up and along the fence. It all just seemed special. And at Christmas, the decorations that sparkled made me believe that someday I could give my life sparkle, too." She shrugged. "Maybe lighting up the park for Christmas will give a child a fantasy of what he can be or do in the future."

They had reached the gazebo now. No one else was in sight.

"You really didn't have a home."

She'd never talked to Zack much about her childhood—she'd just given him bits and pieces. The one thing she'd never wanted was for Zack to feel sorry for her. "Our trailer was a home when Dad was there. It was a home while Mom was alive. It was still a home even when only *I* was by myself...until I got lonely. That's when I'd go looking for a horse to talk to."

Zack stopped, eyed the park again, then responded, "I know what you mean. I did the same thing. After all, I had a lot of horses to choose from, and every one of them had their own personality. I learned that about animals before I learned it about people."

"I won't ask which are easier," she said with a laugh.

"Right. We both know the answer to that one. But once I got my first video camera, I could see more about the horses I videotaped and more about people. I could study them from behind that lens more easily. I became part of the scenery and they forgot I was there. I'd be shooting from across the pasture and Duke's ear would flicker because he knew I was around. Yet he still let me examine the way he related to the other horses, the way he ran, the way he just enjoyed a sunny day."

"I remember Duke. You took him on our rides up to Moonshadow Mountain and Feather Peak."

Zack had been attached to Duke. Was he attached to anyone or anything now?

"Do you have anyone special in your life?" Yes, she wanted to know for her own benefit, but she was concerned about him, too.

He put one gloved hand on the gazebo above her head then stared down at her as if he wanted to decipher where her question came from. Finally, as if he'd come to a decision, he answered her. "No, no one special. I broke it off with a woman I'd been seeing before I came back here for the reunion."

"How long had you been dating?" Her voice held just a slight amount of interest as if his reply didn't matter.

"A couple of months. I think I sensed from the beginning we weren't right together."

She could imagine the dilemma he might face. "How do you know if someone's interested in just you or in what you have? Can you trust your instincts?"

"My gut instinct usually pays off. Sometimes,

though, I ignore it, just to have a little…fun. But there are consequences to every action *and* complications."

She knew all about consequences and complications, possibly even more than Zack did.

He nodded to the folder in Jenny's hand. "So tell me about your ideas for Christmas."

If she could get him interested, would he stay? Hardly. But maybe she *could* get him involved.

Opening the folder, she turned toward one of the lights atop the gazebo. He moved closer to her until he was looking over her shoulder at the folder in her hands. Zack wore a more expensive aftershave than he had when he was a teenager, but she still responded to its woodsy scent. She still got goosebumps when his breath fanned her ear.

She swallowed hard and pointed to her sketch. "We have a couple of women's groups who have volunteered to make evergreen wreaths with candy-cane-striped ribbons. They'd be pretty around the outside of the gazebo. Then I thought we could invest in some of those outdoor flameless candles that have timers. They'd go on every evening at dark and stay lit until midnight. We could actually attach a few of them to the ledge around the gazebo."

"So the gazebo would be like a shelter from the storm."

"Exactly. In the trees around the gazebo, I'd like to arrange those nets of twinkle lights. They'll have their energy sources from the lamp posts."

"Any color at all?"

"I'd like to hang some of those solar balls from the trees. They come in all colors."

"What about vandalism and the chance they'll be stolen?"

She rolled her eyes. "This is Miners Bluff, Zack. Low crime. Noah will put the word out in schools that anyone caught vandalizing will have stiff community service. He's the chief of police now. Did you see him at the reunion?"

"Not much more than a nod and a wave. Maybe I'll have the opportunity to talk to him in the next few weeks."

Noah Stone, one of their classmates, was of Hopi descent. He brought unique sensibilities to his role as chief of police, and the people in town appreciated them.

"You can connect with him tomorrow if you'd like. I got a call from him before we left. He rescued a horse and asked if I'd like to gentle him."

"Do you do that often?"

"Whenever we hear of one in need. Silas let me redo one of the old barns and corrals for that purpose."

Silence met her answer. Finally, he tapped a sketch in her folder. "What's this?"

Putting aside the subject of rescuing horses for the time being, she explained, "I know the private businesses will decorate for Christmas, and have their own lights and garlands. But I'd like to put a star on the courthouse's bell tower. Don't you think that would be a striking touch?"

"The bell still tolls at noon on Saturday?"

"And at midnight on holidays. I thought that star would be a nice reminder of what we're celebrating. Kids need to know Christmas is about more than Santa Claus and presents."

When she closed the folder and turned to face him again, he said, "Kids seem to mean a lot to you."

Her heart hammered. This was a subject she really didn't particularly want to talk about with him. She could give something away too easily. "Kids and Christmas just go together."

"It's more than that. I saw you with them during your riding class. Are you worried your biological clock is ticking?" he asked, half-joking.

"Sure, that's it," she said with a shaky laugh.

He cocked his head as if he knew she wasn't telling him the whole story.

They were the only two people in the park, and the velvet sky and the falling snow created an intimate atmosphere. She gazed up at Zack, seeing the boy he'd been and the man he was now. In spite of her best intentions to keep her distance, both tugged at her heart, created warm tingles on her skin, almost urged her to resurrect the past.

Silver light flickered in his blue eyes and she recognized desire when she saw it. She felt an answering heat in her own body and leaned in a little closer. He braced his hand on the gazebo and leaned into her, too.

The sound of a car horn startled them both.

Quickly, Zack straightened. "We should get over to the town hall." He checked his watch. "Everyone else is probably there by now."

Maybe they were, but she didn't care. She was too busy asking herself what had almost happened. Was Zack about to kiss her? Would she have kissed him back? Her mouth went dry at the thought.

Thank goodness some driver had probably wanted a parking space.

Because one of Zack's kisses could change *everything*.

The following afternoon, Jenny heard the horse trailer roll in and was excited at the prospect of gentling a rescued horse. At least doing this would keep her mind off Zack.

She still wasn't sure whether he would have kissed her at the gazebo. What would have happened if he had? How would she have responded? She hadn't been able to focus at the decorations meeting, and she hadn't slept very much, either. Just having Zack in the house made her edgy.

So this morning she'd done something she might come to regret. She'd asked Brody Hazlett to the dance at the firehouse's social hall on Friday night. Needing more distance between her and Zack, she thought this date might do it. After all, Brody had asked her out before, though she'd always come up with a reason to decline his invitation. Although he was an attractive, down-to-earth guy who loved animals as much as she did—he was a veterinarian—her heart didn't race at the sight of him like it had—and still did—with Zack.

Leaving the tack room in the barn, she went outside and let the November breeze brush her face. She headed for the smaller barn that she'd refurbished to house horses who had been mistreated. There were only four stalls. The doors to those stalls could be opened to a corral that gave plenty of room to horses who wanted to be free. When they felt safer, they could enter the stall.

Today, Noah Stone was bringing her a gelding named Dusty. She didn't know what to expect. She never did. This was one of those situations that had to be taken moment by moment.

To her surprise, as she walked to the corral gate, Zack was standing by the driver side of the truck talking to Noah. They'd been classmates once, but Zack and Noah hadn't run in the same crowd. But time and age were great equalizers and the two men seemed friendly now.

As she approached them, Noah sent her a smile. Zack's expression was neutral.

Noah said, "I was telling Zack I'm often the one who gets called when someone around here sees a horse being mistreated."

"You said Dusty was malnourished?" Zack asked.

"That and other things. I had a time of it getting him into the trailer. I had to use blinders. I don't think he's the type of horse who's going to want to be in a confined space."

"Any history?" Zack inquired, obviously interested.

"Just what I told you. The rancher bought him at an auction, fell on hard times and couldn't feed him. He tried to ride him, but Dusty wasn't cooperative."

"I don't think I want to know any more," Jenny said. "I don't think I *need* to know any more."

Zack had been taking in their conversation. "Getting him out shouldn't be a problem. But leading him where you want him to go might be something else."

"I'll open the gate and you can back the trailer in," Jenny informed Noah.

Zack's gaze met Jenny's, and she felt a shiver run down her spine that wasn't from the cold.

After another look that made Jenny remember the closeness of their bodies last night all over again, Zack motioned Noah through the gate opening into the corral.

As Noah backed up the truck and trailer, Zack asked her, "Does Noah's father still have horses?"

"A few. But he's had some health problems and Noah has been helping him with the chores on their ranch."

Once Noah stopped and climbed out of the truck, Zack suggested, "Why don't I go inside and back him out."

For a moment, Jenny felt indignant. "I'm fully capable of doing this, Zack."

"I have no doubt you are. I just thought you might want to take the blinders off."

He *was* right about that.

"All right. Thanks," she murmured, knowing she couldn't be so touchy around Zack. That would tip him off that her feelings were more personal than she wanted to admit.

After Noah opened the back of the horse trailer, he lowered the ramp. "Okay, Zack," he called.

Inside the trailer, Zack called back, "Give me a few minutes, okay?"

"If he thinks he's going to sweet-talk him," Noah said with a shake of his head, "he's sadly mistaken."

"I don't think it's sweet talk. Maybe Zack just wants to get him used to a kind voice."

As she and Noah waited, she wondered if Zack still had "the touch." He'd been so good at handling horses as a kid. But mishandled horses were another matter. It could take many months to calm Dusty down, many months to establish trust. Even the training she did with cutting horses was all about forming a relationship. She'd learned *that* from Noah Stone's father and grandfather. She'd worked there one summer when she was fifteen and learned lessons she'd keep for a lifetime. Not lessons about not owning a horse, but becoming friends with a horse, about not expecting a horse to listen like a human, but about creating communication bonds both she and the animal would understand.

Horses had herd instincts. She had to become leader of their herd of two—a kind leader but a confident, firm leader. She'd had to *learn* her skills, but Zack seemed to have been born with them.

Zack called, "I'm going to back him out."

As soon as the horse's back legs were off the ramp, he was kicking out, pulling at the lead, defying everyone around him. Zack held on and wouldn't let him rear up.

"Blinders off," he called to Noah and Jenny. "They're driving him crazy."

Before Noah could move, Jenny had slipped up beside Zack, unfastened the blinders and let them drop into her hands. All the while, Zack kept a firm hand on the lead and spoke in gentle tones.

Jenny could have cried. Dusty, a buff-colored gelding with a black mane and tail, was trembling. She felt so sorry for him. Yet she knew she couldn't get too close too fast. She knew she had to bide her time. The horse's gaze couldn't seem to settle anywhere.

Zack suggested, "You and Noah drop back. Let me lead him in."

The horse had stopped kicking, though he was dancing around, moving fretfully. Jenny knew better than to try and touch him yet. She had to let him come to her.

"All right," she said. "Noah, do you think you can ease out of the gate? Once I close it, Zack, you can take off the lead and let him run free."

Jenny held her breath as Noah eased the truck out of the corral. Dusty tried to rear up but Zack held the lead and his strength was obvious.

As quietly as possible, as slowly as possible, she shut the gate.

Zack asked, "Are you going into the barn?"

She knew he wanted her to, but that wasn't going to happen. "No, I'll just climb to the other side of the fence. Are you sure *you* want to do this? As soon as you let go, he might become even wilder."

"It's okay, Dusty. No one's going to hurt you." Zack's voice was almost hypnotic. In the same tone he assured her, "I'll be fine. I'll see what he does when I unhook the lead."

Scaling the fence to the outside of the corral, Jenny watched as Zack continued to talk to Dusty in the same low tones, as he tried to keep the horse's attention focused on him, as he tried to start building trust.

He reached toward the fastener slowly, unhooked it and stood perfectly still. For a second or two, Dusty didn't seem to know what to do. But then he snorted, pawed and kicked up his back legs again.

Jenny was afraid he might simply gallop into Zack. But Zack just stood there, speaking softly, not moving a muscle, until finally Dusty wheeled in the other direction and ran like the devil was chasing him to the other end of the corral. Zack took that opportunity to cross quickly to the fence, climb up and settle on the top rung.

Dusty ran across the corral, aimed straight for him, then at the last moment veered away, running again.

Looking up at Zack, she murmured, "You took a chance."

"Better me than you," he muttered.

"Don't turn protective on me, Zack. You've no right."

He climbed down off the fence to stand before her and look her straight in the eye. "Yes, I do. My father depends on you. I'll do what I have to do to keep you safe."

Maybe he'd keep her physically safe, but he couldn't keep her heart safe.

"Come on," he said. "Let's watch him from the barn. You don't even have your jacket on."

She was about to protest she was wearing an insulated vest, but knew that would do no good. She *was* cold, now that the adrenaline had stopped rushing.

They hurried to the side door and Zack let her precede him into the barn. Her arm brushed against his sheepskin jacket, but she didn't look up at him. She didn't want to remember that moment last night when they'd stood so near, their breathing synchronized—

Taking her phone from her pocket, she speed-dialed Noah. "Thanks. Do you want to come up to the house for lunch? Martha probably has it ready."

"No, thanks, Jenny. I have to get back to my office to handle paperwork."

"You spend your life there."

He laughed. "It's my job. I don't tell you that you spend too many hours working, do I?"

"That's because you know it wouldn't do any good."

"Right."

"I'll accept your refusal this time," she conceded.

"But let's just say I owe you lunch. Thanks again." After Noah said goodbye, she closed her phone and stuck it back in her pocket.

Zack said, "You and Noah are friends," as if he were confirming something in his mind.

"Yes, we are."

"He's very different now than he was in high school," Zack decided. "He's confident, not rebellious and defiant."

"I never would have thought he would have gone into law enforcement, but he had his reasons," Jenny responded. "Training and working in the Phoenix police department changed his outlook on a lot of things."

"I can imagine," Zack said, as if he could.

She didn't know why she'd thought Zack had no empathy left anymore. Maybe because he'd put up a barrier between himself and his dad that was so high neither of them could breach it. Yet, she was seeing now that barrier didn't necessarily define Zack's character any more than it defined Silas's.

Crossing to the feed bins, Zack picked up two wreaths of golden bells that were lying there. "I haven't seen these for years."

"You remember them?"

"How can I not? My mother loved bells, especially at Christmas—sleigh bells, garlands with bells, wreaths with bells."

There was such fondness and affection in Zack's voice, Jenny was drawn toward him. "And red velvet ribbon," she added. "She tied big red bows on anything to do with Christmas."

"What are you going to do with these?" he asked, a bit roughly.

"I hang them on the barn doors, just like she did. Then we hear the jingle of bells up at the house. It's a nice sound when the wind is howling or when the snow is falling."

"I didn't know you'd kept up some of her traditions."

"If you would have come home—"

The look he gave her made her cut off her words. "I loved your mom, Zack, and I want to keep remembering her. We put up a Christmas tree and I use the ornaments she collected over the years. She had favorite recipes for the holidays and I made sure Martha makes those. Your father wants to remember, too."

An almost angry look shone in Zack's eyes. "Don't tell me he loved her. He couldn't have loved her and treated her the way he did."

Instead of heading into the eye of *that* storm, Jenny asked, "Do you know how your parents met?"

He thought about it. "Her father was buying her a cutting horse as a birthday present."

"Your grandfather had recently died and your dad was trying to keep the Rocky D afloat," she said, filling him in.

"I remember Mom talking about those years," Zack responded, a far-away look in his eyes.

"From what I understand, your grandfather had let it go south," Jenny explained. "Your dad took over, had a couple of bad years but managed to turn it around by expanding the breeding facilities and the training opportunities. That's when everything took off for him. But at the beginning..."

"At the beginning, what?" Zack seemed genuinely curious.

"Picture this, Zack. This beautiful, raven-haired

woman with more poise than any model comes to the Rocky D with her very rich father. Your mom had received her college education back East and was going to teach at Northern Arizona University. Your father, to his way of thinking, had gotten through high school the best way he could, with no real love for books. He was scrimping to pay the bills. Yet the two of them, as different as they were, were drawn to each other."

"What are you trying to tell me, Jenny? That my father felt inferior to my mother?"

"I think he did…in a lot of ways."

"That doesn't excuse the gambling and the affairs. Was he trying to prove he could become richer easily? Was he trying to prove he was deserving of her somehow, because other women wanted him, too? That doesn't make any sense."

"It might not make sense to *us*. But to a man in his position back then, maybe it did. It's not an excuse. But it might be a reason. When a man doesn't feel worthy, his world is pretty lopsided."

"What was my mother supposed to do? Disown her family? Pretend she wasn't educated?"

"I'm not saying there was a solution, Zack. But maybe if they'd understood each other better, talked more, realized each other's fears, your dad wouldn't have been so obsessed with becoming a giant in the community any way he could."

"My mother should have left him. She wouldn't be dead if she'd walked away."

"And what would she have done about *you?*" Jenny protested. "Would she have taken you with her? Would she have left you with your father? If she took you, would she be denying you your birthright? Denying you the Rocky D and everything it represented? There's no easy decision for a mother in that position."

He was looking at her as if he was trying to figure her out. "You sound like you know."

She shook her head but couldn't take her gaze from his.

He was leaning toward her slightly, one hand over the back of the stall, the other free to do whatever it wanted. She suddenly wanted his arms around her. She suddenly wanted a lot more than that.

As if he was reading the message in her eyes, he did put his arm around her—and he bent his head to hers.

The first touch of Zack's lips wasn't anything like Jenny expected. She'd expected hard, possessive and arrogant. His lips were firm as if he knew what he wanted. But they were coaxing, too…encouraging her to respond. If she had thought further than that, she might have saved them both a lot of trouble. But she didn't, because all of her concentration was on the feel of his mouth, the touch of his tongue against hers, the strength of his arms as he pulled her closer, enveloping her fully in his embrace.

She couldn't fall in love with Zack again. She couldn't let her future be affected like that again. She *wouldn't.*

Wrenching away, she looked up at him and shook her head. "No. You're not going to make me want you and then turn around and leave again. It won't happen, Zack. I won't let it. I deserve more than that."

Without waiting for a response from him, she returned outside to watch Dusty. If Zack built any sense of trust with this horse, it would be broken when he left.

Neither of them needed Zack Decker, and she'd better not forget that.

Chapter Five

At midnight, Zack stood on the back veranda of the
east wing overlooking the rose garden. A frosting of
snow coated the bare branches of the bushes that slept
during the winter. This had been his mother's favorite
spot. Her rosebushes had been her pride and joy. He
wondered if Jenny collected blooms, in colors from
yellow and coral to light pink and magenta, for each of
the downstairs rooms as his mother had.

No matter how much he wanted to forget it, he could
taste Jenny's kiss on his lips. He'd been reckless and
impulsive in the barn, two qualities that hadn't been
part of his life as an adult. But Jenny had always turned
him inside out. Most of all, she made him *feel*. As a kid,
he'd turned off his feelings as his parents fought. He'd
turned off his feelings when Jenny had decided not to
go with him to L.A. He'd turned off his feelings in any-

thing that approached business. In all these years, he'd only let them free when he was behind the lens.

When he heard the French doors open and close, he almost exhaled a frustrated breath. He knew the sound of that heavy tread. "You shouldn't be out here, Dad. It's too cold. You don't want to overtax—"

"Stow it," his father mumbled. "I needed some fresh air."

"At midnight?"

His father came to stand beside him, looking out at the garden. "I'm feeling claustrophobic. A man's not made to be cooped up in the house."

"It's not for long. As soon as you're feeling stronger you can walk wherever you want. Just don't push it."

Instead of reacting to Zack's words, Silas gestured to the fountain in the middle of the rose garden. "Jenny put in one of those solar fountains. She prunes the rosebushes herself. She won't let anyone else near them."

"I don't see how she has time for that with everything else she takes care of."

"That girl has energy. Always has."

"She's not a girl anymore."

After a few moments of quiet, Silas asked, "Do you ever regret what you left behind?"

Zack wasn't sure how to answer that one. Certainly his father didn't want to get into an argument about anything that had happened. He kept his answer simple.

"I don't have regrets about leaving. I had to find out who I was without the Decker name and wealth. You never understood that."

"Maybe I understood more than you thought. Maybe I hated that camera of yours because I knew it would take you away from here."

Which, of course, it had.

"And what about Jenny?" his father asked gruffly. "Do you wish you had taken her along?"

Zack felt more than saw his father turn toward him and study him in the shadows. He wasn't about to start confiding in a man who might use those confidences against him.

At Zack's silence, Silas grunted. "She hasn't told you everything yet, has she?"

Nothing else could have gotten his attention as that did. "What are you talking about?"

"You need to ask Jenny that yourself. Did she happen to mention she's going with Brody Hazlett to the dance at the fire hall Friday night?"

Zack didn't want to admit he knew nothing about the dance or about Jenny and Brody Hazlett. Except that they'd been dancing together at the reunion when he'd cut in. "No."

"Apparently, a lot of your old classmates will be there. Jenny's friends for sure. You can buy a ticket at the door...if you're interested."

Was he interested? If not in the dance, in finding out if anything was going on between Jenny and Brody?

Zack let his pride slip a little and asked, "Has she been dating him?"

"Nope. He's asked but she always says no. I don't know what happened to change her mind." Silas coughed, then coughed again. "I guess I've had enough of this air. I'll see you in the morning."

Zack almost caught his dad's arm...almost asked, *What hasn't Jenny told me?*...almost felt something more than the bitterness and resentment toward his father that he'd nurtured all these years.

But he didn't ask. He just said, "Good night, Dad."

He heard the French doors close behind his father. Zack was an outsider here and he'd never felt more like one than he did tonight.

A harvest theme prevailed in the fire hall Friday evening. Stacked bales of hay were supposed to give the room a barnlike ambience. A section of rustic fencing had even been set up along one side of what was supposed to be the dance floor. A fiddle was playing now, a man on a mike called out square dancing moves. Zack hadn't been square dancing since high school, and he doubted that he even remembered how.

So what the hell was he doing here?

That was a no-brainer. He spotted Jenny easily in a red checked blouse and denim skirt, do-si-do-ing with Brody. He'd thought about his father's words all last night and all today. *She hasn't told you everything yet, has she?* What exactly did Jenny have to tell him? Or was his father just causing trouble?

Zack had spent a good part of the day with Dusty, just talking to him, letting the horse get used to the sound of his voice. When Jenny had come around at lunchtime to tell him she'd take over, he'd let her, without any conversation. He wasn't sure what he wanted to say to her, and she was just as awkward with him. Awkward or not, he wanted to kiss her again. But she wasn't coming too close and he knew that was for the best. Had she come to the dance tonight to put another wall between them? Or was she really interested in Brody?

What did he care when he wouldn't be staying?

He knew already he couldn't spend the evening

watching her. Clay and Celeste, who were seated at one of the long, red cloth-covered tables, waved and motioned to him. Zack smiled as he studied the couple. They were newlyweds and anyone could tell. Seated close together, shoulders touching, their hands entwined on the table.

A few of the townsfolk recognized him, smiled and nodded as he crossed to his classmates. One called out, "I hope your dad's back on his feet soon," and another said, "Good to see you're back." There were no gawkers here as he might have encountered in L.A. if anyone had recognized him. That was one benefit to being in Miners Bluff. He felt ordinary again. To his surprise, he actually enjoyed that feeling.

The fiddling was loud and Zack knew conversation would be tough. He went to the Sullivans' side of the table and stood between them. "You two look happy."

"Life is good," Clay said with a satisfied smile. "How's your dad?"

"As ornery as ever. Liam O'Rourke came over to visit with him tonight. Martha was still there, too, so I know he's being watched over." He tapped his phone in the pocket of his shirt. "He has my number on speed dial, but he'd probably call Jenny if there was an emergency."

The three of them glanced over to where she was still dancing with Brody, her blond ponytail swinging with the music, her skirt flaring out around her when she moved.

After Celeste and Clay exchanged a look, Celeste said, "You'll have to stop over when you get a chance. I could make dinner. I'm sure my cooking isn't what you're used to, but we'd love to have you."

"I do a lot of take-out," Zack responded with a wry grin. "I'll give you a call when Dad's feeling better. I'm not going to stay very long tonight."

Mikala Conti suddenly appeared at Zack's side. "It's good to see you here."

"Hi, Mik. How's your aunt?"

"She's good. She'd be here tonight but she has a cold she's trying to beat."

Zack had always liked Mikala. With her wavy black hair and tobacco-brown eyes, she had quiet beauty and listening skills that made her easy to talk to. He wondered if she knew more about Jenny and Brody.

As the fiddling stopped, the announcer let everyone know they were slowing things down with an old Patsy Cline standard. Zack suddenly asked Mikala, "Would you like to dance?"

She was totally surprised for a few seconds, and then smiled. "Sure."

"Talk to you later," he said to Clay and Celeste, as he led Mikala to the dance floor. Mikala waved to Riley O'Rourke and Noah who were standing by the snack table talking to Katie Paladin, another of their classmates.

"Almost like the reunion," Mikala said with a smile, as Zack put his arm around her and took her hand in the standard ballroom position. Mikala *was* a beautiful woman, but Zack didn't feel the attraction he'd felt with Jenny when he held her in his arms. Lust that had started as a teenager shouldn't still be alive fifteen years later! But it was, and he couldn't help glancing toward Jenny again. She and Brody were dancing close, and Zack's gut clenched.

"Earth to Zack," Mikala called softly.

Feeling embarrassment for the first time in a long time, Zack brought his attention back to his dance partner. "Sorry. What did I miss?"

Mikala laughed softly and shook her head. "I asked if you heard from Dawson lately? At the reunion, he told me the two of you kept in touch."

"Actually, I did. Did you know he's thinking of moving back here? In fact, he's pretty sure about it."

"Is he really going to do it?" Mikala's eyes seemed to take on an extra sparkle and Zack wondered about that. He didn't remember Dawson and Mikala being an item in high school. Dawson had hung out with everyone at Mikala's aunt's but also dated the popular girls. Zack didn't think Dawson and Mikala had been more than friends. But what did he know? He'd been too smitten with Jenny.

"If he moves back here, I think you're one of the reasons," Zack admitted to Mikala. "He thinks you might be able to help Luke."

The sparkle left Mikala's eyes and her expression became more polite than friendly. Zack guessed why. "You can't talk about that, can you? Because of patient confidentiality?"

"That's right."

Zack knew he could hold his own on the dance floor. He had to for all the social functions he attended. He took Mikala through a few intricate steps and found her to be an excellent partner. "I should have known you'd be good at dancing. After all, you're all about music."

"Music has been my salvation on many an occasion." She tilted her head and eyed him thoughtfully. "Just as film-making has been yours."

This close friend of Jenny's understood more than he expected. "Was I so transparent as a teenager?"

"No, not to everyone. Maybe I just understood because I used music to escape the same way you used that video camera. Besides, even now I can see the intensity and desire to make the world a better place in your films. Jenny and I have talked about that."

"You have?" He kept his voice neutral, not knowing if he wanted to know what Mikala and Jenny spoke about concerning his films and his life.

When he glanced toward Jenny and Brody again, he saw they were laughing, seemingly having a good time. As he turned away from them and Mikala caught sight of them, she said, "Jenny and Brody are friends."

"The way you and I are friends?"

"Possibly. Brody spends some time at the Rocky D treating the horses."

"It's none of my business," Zack muttered, knowing it wasn't, yet feeling pangs of jealousy anyway. He might as well call a spade a spade.

Mikala's understanding expression told him he wasn't fooling her one bit.

After the ballad ended, Zack escorted Mikala back to where Celeste and Clay were seated. He sat with them for a while, listening to the women describe Celeste and Clay's wedding. He couldn't help being cynical about marriage. Years ago, he'd decided he'd *never* marry. He never wanted to end up the way his mom and dad had, fighting all the time, looking at each other with resentment, playing the social game for others to see. Yet Clay and Celeste certainly seemed happy. The way they spoke about their daughter and their life together gave Zack pause.

After another hour chatting with people, he decided to call it a night. He had to admit, reconnecting with old friends had been enjoyable. Yet his gaze had never been far from Jenny and he was on edge about her relationship with Brody. After he retrieved his jacket and hat from a rack, he exited through a side door. Shoving his hands into his jacket pockets, he took a few deep breaths and gazed up at the night sky. This wasn't a smog-filled California sky. It was a Miners Bluff sky, with too many stars to count.

When he rounded the side of the building to head to the parking lot, he heard voices around the corner— Jenny's and Brody's.

She said, "Thanks for coming with me tonight."

"You surprised me when you called. The last couple of times I asked you out you were busy."

Zack didn't hear Jenny's answer to that. He didn't *want* to hear it. What if she said her feelings toward him had changed and she was interested in dating him for a while, to see how their relationship would progress? After all, isn't that what she should do? Especially if she wanted to have a family.

Zack strode through the parking lot, his thoughts all in a jumble. He shouldn't care. He didn't care. Yet he remembered Mikala's knowing look. He knew denial was a strong defense against unwanted feelings.

His life was in California and Jenny had no desire to leave Miners Bluff. Those were the same facts that had divided them once before.

Back at the ranch a half hour later, Zack checked on his father. Silas was sleeping. In the kitchen, Martha was setting the table for breakfast. Now that Zack was home, she went to her quarters without worrying Silas might need her. Zack thanked her for looking after his father, then made a pot of coffee, expecting to be up for a while. He had work to do and he was always productive at night.

He'd just poured himself a mug of the freshly brewed coffee when Jenny came in the side door from the garage. She looked startled to see him standing there.

"Decaf?" she asked, nodding toward the coffee pot.

"Nope. I found the real thing in the freezer."

She laughed, but it was an uncomfortable laugh. An I-know-there's-something-we-need-to-talk-about laugh. Except she tried to exit the kitchen so quickly, he understood she didn't want to talk. Tough. He did.

"Jenny?" he called before she was through the doorway.

She stopped but she obviously didn't want to. "It's late, Zack. I have an early morning. I need to exercise a few of the horses in the arena before Michael and Tanya come for their lesson."

He took a moment to absorb that. "I was going to work with Dusty, but if you need my help—"

"I don't."

The tension between them pulled taut.

She added, "If he learns to trust you and then you leave, I'm not sure your time with him is going to be beneficial."

"If he learns to trust me and then I leave, he'll have learned at least one human being can be kind to him. I don't see that it will hurt, as long as you work with him, too."

Jenny kept silent, but unbuttoned her turquoise-and-red-patterned wool jacket. He might as well ask her what was on his mind. "So are you and Hazlett going to see each other now?"

Her eyebrows quirked up. "What gave you that idea?"

"You seemed to be having a good time with him."

"Brody and I go back a ways, Zack. We're friends. That's it. I pretty much told him that tonight."

"You did?"

"Yes."

"I accidentally overheard some of your conversation with him before I left the fire hall. Why did you ask him to the dance? Why didn't you just ask me to take you? Aren't *we* friends, Jenny?"

She didn't answer him and that bothered him more than he wanted to admit. So he left his mug on the counter and crossed to her. "Dad and I had a conversation the other night."

He could see she was listening wholeheartedly now, wondering what was coming next. He wondered the same thing. "You know how he likes to make cryptic comments. He said to me, 'She hasn't told you everything yet, has she?' and I asked him what he meant. He wouldn't answer. He said I should ask you."

Jenny suddenly looked panicked, just like Dusty did sometimes when he was cornered…when Zack approached him and he wasn't sure what Zack would do.

Zack reached out and took Jenny by the shoulders, partly to comfort her, partly because he wanted to know the truth. Had she been married and divorced in the fifteen years he'd been away? Did something happen to her while he was gone?

He had no idea what to expect. He certainly didn't expect the tears that came to Jenny's eyes, and her attempt to pull away.

"Jenny, what's going on? What was Dad talking about?"

Her lower lip quivering, but her head held high, she finally answered him. "I found out I was pregnant after you left. Six weeks later, I had a miscarriage."

Although Zack heard the words, it took a few moments for their full impact to hit him. He was stunned by the thought of Jenny being pregnant—and even more stunned that she hadn't told him.

"Tell me what happened." Emotion filled his voice—he couldn't seem to hold in the turmoil Jenny was creating.

Her face went pale as if she hadn't expected him to ask that. Her eyes looked for an escape, but there was none because he wouldn't let her turn away from him. She confessed, "I had a fall."

He guessed right away. "From a horse?"

"Yes."

"My God! Why did my parents let you ride?"

"Only your mom knew. Your dad didn't until the day I fell."

"Why were you riding when you were pregnant?"

"I couldn't quit my job here. I needed the money."

"The money? You lost our baby because of money?"

Her eyes flashed and her whole body tensed. "Don't sound so self-righteous, Zack. You don't have the right. You left."

"Why didn't you tell me?" The question came slowly because he had such a hard time getting it out. He was filled with anger and disappointment and loss.

"I didn't tell you so you could chase your dream. I didn't want to be a burden on you or hold you back. I didn't want you to resent me for trapping you."

The reasons spilled out of her as if she'd been holding them in for fifteen years. He supposed she had. "Did you know before I left?"

"Not until a few weeks after. Your mom saw me throwing up behind the barn one day and she guessed. She tried to convince me to tell you, and I was going to, but then I lost the baby and there just didn't seem to be any point."

Everything she was revealing swirled in his head. Looking at her, at the face that had been in his dreams more times than he could ever count, he saw the honesty he'd always expected from Jenny. Yet she'd kept this secret for *fifteen* years.

"Who else knew?" he asked, feeling betrayed.

"No one else. Only your parents...and a doctor your mom took me to."

No wonder Jenny and his mother had been so close. They'd had this secret between them as well as everything else. If only she'd told him. If only he could have been here for her. He murmured, "I can't believe you never told me."

She must have taken his complete shock at her disclosure as an accusation, because she asked, "How was I supposed to tell you, Zack, when you were miles away in a different life? What happened didn't matter anymore. I was young and stupid and devastated when you left. Along with that, I had to get over losing a baby. It wasn't as if you came home or wrote or phoned. Your parents and I were just part of your old life. We didn't matter anymore."

He wanted to deny that, but he'd embraced his future with all the energy he'd possessed, leaving behind his father's disapproval and Jenny's refusal to go with him. Yet she said she'd been *devastated* by his leaving. It all seemed so incomprehensible now.

"What happened mattered," he protested. "The fact you were carrying my baby *mattered*. The loss of our child *matters*. It's true, I don't know what I would have done. But I wish I'd had the chance to find out."

Now when Jenny tried to pull away, he didn't hold her. He couldn't bear gazing into her brown eyes, filled with the pain of what she'd experienced.

As she left him in the kitchen, her pain gripped him and became his.

Chapter Six

After Zack had spent some time with Dusty, he had gone on a cold morning ride, trying to sort out everything Jenny had told him last night. He'd stayed up most of the night, lost in the past, remembering too much about their senior year in high school, remembering too much about the night he and Jenny had made love in the hayloft. He'd been naive back then, more experienced physically than emotionally. He'd believed that night had meant as much to her as it had meant to him. He had to admit that he'd been bitter and resentful about her refusal to go with him ever since. But now—

Returning to the Rocky D after a fast ride he'd hoped would numb his thoughts, he spotted Jenny entering the arena with Michael and his sister.

As he lead Tattoo into the everyday barn, Hank saw him and waved. "I'll take him for you if you'd like."

"Are you sure?" Zack asked. "I know you have enough to do." Hank was a few years younger than Silas but never seemed to slow down.

"No problem. I see how much time you're spending with Dusty. He won't let me get anywhere near him."

"We'll have to change that. Maybe tomorrow if you have a little time, you could come with me and I'll show you some of the things I've learned about him."

"Like?" Hank asked with an arched brow.

"Like if you sit on the fence long enough, he'll come over to see what you're about."

"*You,* not me."

"We just have to show him there are a lot more nice humans in the world than cruel ones."

Hank laughed and shook his head. "You never *would* believe you had a special gift. But I'll come out with you tomorrow in that dang cold just to prove my point."

Zack shook Hank's hand and agreed, "It's a deal." Then he left Tattoo with a man he'd learned to trust when he was just a boy.

Zack took out his cell phone as he strode to the arena and speed-dialed his father.

Silas picked up on the second ring. "Where are you?" his father asked without any preamble.

"I'm going to the arena to see what Jenny's up to. I just thought I'd check in, to see if you needed anything."

"I need some energy and a good dose of stamina."

"When are you coming down to the barn?" His dad had been walking on the paved paths in back of the house. He also now climbed the stairs to his bedroom each night. That was progress even though his dad didn't seem to see it that way. But he hadn't taken a stroll down to the barns yet and it was time.

The silence was so lengthy, Zack asked, "Dad?"

"Not when there are people around. Jenny's got those kids there and their mom will be coming to pick them up. Ben went to Flagstaff today but Hank and Tate are around somewhere, too."

"What are you afraid will happen?"

"I'm not afraid of anything."

Becoming more comfortable at the Rocky D again, Zack had forgotten he needed to watch his words. "What are you *concerned* might happen?"

"I can't *do* what I used to do. I don't know when I'll be riding again and I don't want anybody asking me about it. Jenny said something about going to lunch with Mikala and Celeste on Monday. Hank will be going into town to place a feed order. The temporary hands won't care what I'm doing. Maybe then I'll take a walk over."

"All right, whenever you want. You know what the doctor said—build up each day."

"Go do what you gotta do," Silas muttered. "I'm fine here for now." Then his father hung up.

Go do what he had to do. Talk to Jenny about what had happened fifteen years ago? Not likely with two kids around. Yet he felt drawn to the arena where he knew she'd be.

Opening the heavy door, he stepped inside. Jenny was riding Goldenrod, one of the horses she'd be putting up for sale in the spring. Michael and Tanya were following her in a circle on two of the mares Jenny trusted with kids. One of them, a chestnut with a white blaze, was her own horse—Songbird.

He heard Michael say, "I wish we could come out here and ride every day."

Zack heard Jenny laugh, a sweet sound he'd always

enjoyed. She responded, "You have to go to school, and I have horses to train."

"It's great you have an arena," he said. "That way if it snows, we can still ride."

"That was the idea when Mr. Decker built it."

After a few moments, Tanya informed her, "Daddy doesn't like when we come here."

"That's just because he can't pay," Michael explained. "I heard him arguing with Mom again about taking handouts. He doesn't want anything for free."

Jenny stopped leading and waited until Michael brought his horse up beside hers. "Your mom will be here shortly. Let's dismount and unsaddle. If we have time, you can help me groom."

Jenny dismounted first and then helped both of the kids. As Zack watched her, he realized she was as gentle as a caring mother. Last night, when she'd told him about the miscarriage, there had been such sadness in her voice. Did she long to have children now? Did she want a family?

As they walked the horses to their stalls along the edge of the arena, Zack joined them, ready to help with their saddles.

"Hi, guys."

"Hi, Mr. Decker," Michael said, as Tanya grinned shyly. "Carson and Danielle couldn't come, so it's just us today! I was hoping I'd see you," Michael went on. "Can I talk to you?"

Jenny gave Zack a look that asked what it was about, but Zack shrugged, having no idea. Their gazes stayed connected longer than necessary, but then she broke eye contact and almost too eagerly helped Tanya. Michael joined Zack by a set of feed bins.

"What's up?" Zack asked.

"You know how to make movies."

Zack suppressed a smile. "Does making movies interest you?"

"Not really. I mean, I don't want to make a movie exactly. I want to make a video of me and Tanya to give to my mom and dad for Christmas. My mom said we're going to have to be inventive this year and think of things to give each other that don't cost money. Well, my dad has a video camera and there's some blank tapes with it he never used. So I thought it would be really cool if you could help me and Tanya make a movie for Mom and Dad. What do you think?"

The last thing Zack was thinking about was the holidays. He was obviously going to be here for Thanksgiving. But Christmas? That was still up for grabs. He thought about what Michael had said, about the family being inventive so they could give each other gifts that didn't cost anything. Wasn't *that* a novel concept? He didn't give many Christmas gifts. For the most part, Christmas was just another day. He remembered again how special the holidays had been to his mother.

He didn't know why he was even considering this boy's request. It wasn't something he'd ever do if he was back in L.A. But the sparkling hope in Michael's eyes, the idea his parents would derive joy from this present that was much needed in their lives encouraged Zack to say, "Let me think about the best way to do it. Can you get the camera here without your parents knowing?"

"Sure. I can put it in my backpack. It's a little heavy, but not that big. It has real small tapes."

Zack understood exactly what kind of camcorder Michael was talking about. "We have some time. Christmas is still weeks away. Bring the camcorder along next Saturday when you come. Maybe Jenny can tell your mom the lesson's going to run longer than usual. That way we'll have a chance after the other kids leave. Okay?"

Michael was beaming. "I can't believe you said yes."

"Why is that?"

"Because my dad said you're really an important person and you're not going to be here long. He said you're just here because your dad's sick, and then you'll fly off and not be seen for another five to ten years."

Zack was used to tabloid news about him, rumors that weren't true, stories that were exaggerated from the telling. He knew there had to be gossip around Miners Bluff about his return. Apparently, this was some of it.

"I won't be here too long," he told Michael. "But I'll be here long enough to help you make a present for your parents. That's a promise."

"Cool!" Michael grinned from ear to ear.

Zack felt good about his decision, better than he'd felt about anything in a while.

As Michael and Tanya groomed their horses, chattering away as they did, Zack approached Jenny. She was running the grooming brush over her horse's back.

"Can you tell Michael's mother that their lesson will run longer next week?"

Jenny didn't look at him as she asked, "Why?"

"Because I'm going to help him with something after the other kids leave."

Now she did turn her gaze up to his. "Zack, they're under my care. You're going to have to tell me what you're planning."

"What do you think I'm going to do, take them on a

trail ride to Feather Peak in the snow?" He didn't know why her lack of trust made him angry, but it did.

She sighed and turned to face him. "Does it have to be a secret?"

"No. Michael wants me to help shoot footage of him and his sister as a present for their parents for Christmas. That's it. Nothing nefarious."

"And you said *yes?*" She seemed really surprised and that did nothing to take the edge off his annoyance with her attitude.

"I said *yes.* What do you think happened to me in L.A., Jenny? Do you think I became a different person than the one you knew?"

She looked over at the kids to make sure they weren't listening. They weren't. They were engrossed in what they were doing and talking with each other. "All I know is that you left and didn't look back."

Stiffening, he kept a lid on his temper, remembering what had happened to her and the pain he'd glimpsed in her eyes. "Last night, fifteen years after the fact, you told me why I should have looked back. I wasn't a mind reader, Jenny. I didn't know what was happening back here. Obviously, you didn't want me to know. I stayed in touch with my mother. I would have stayed in touch with you if you'd given me any indication you wanted that. But you didn't. So tell me who's to blame in all this."

"We can't talk now," she said in a whisper.

"Do you want to make an appointment?"

"Zack—"

The arena door opened and Helen Larson walked in. She called, "Michael, Tanya. I'm here."

Zack realized his moment with Jenny had been lost again.

Jenny said in a low voice, "I'll tell her the lessons will last longer next week. We can talk later."

Jenny said the words, but when Zack studied her face, he saw she didn't want to talk later any more than she did now. Would they accomplish anything at all if they spoke about what had happened? Or would speaking about the past widen the gap between them?

Late that night, Zack finally got a private moment with Jenny.

She'd eluded him all day, but she wasn't going to elude him now. He stood outside her bedroom door and knocked.

"Zack!" She looked startled when she opened her door.

She was already dressed for bed in a flannel nightgown that on anybody else might not look enticing, but on her, the pink background and small flowers, the short ruffle around the neck, the way the flannel lay over her breasts was alluring.

"Can I come in?"

"I'm ready for bed. I have an early day tomorrow."

"We need to talk, Jenny, about a couple of things. I really don't want Dad to overhear us so I thought your room would be best." He was now ensconced in his old room near his dad's master suite.

After a moment's hesitation, Jenny backed up and let him inside. She was the type of woman who toughed things out. She'd make a point, even though she might be uncomfortable doing it. The point tonight was—she could stand in her flannel nightgown in front of him and not look nervous.

The gas fireplace in her room was lit and she settled on the mauve and sage-green, flowered sofa, pulling the pale pink afghan from the back and covering herself with it. The room was a little chilly, but he doubted if Jenny would have used that afghan if she were alone.

Whatever. This wasn't a date. He sat down on the sofa about a foot away from her. Her gaze swept over him. He was wearing a navy flannel shirt, jeans and boots, usual attire for the ranch in the winter. He couldn't tell what she was thinking, but her gaze on him made him feel much too warm.

"Did you know Dad invested in a horse farm in Kentucky?" he asked.

That obviously wasn't a question she'd been expecting. "Yes, I knew. Why?"

Her surprise kept her from being defensive and he was glad of that. "Because it's losing money faster than any of the thoroughbreds they're raising there can run a mile."

She gave a small shrug. "He didn't invest in it just to make money."

Zack narrowed his eyes. "Why did he invest?"

"Because the family owned the ranch for generations. It's been going downhill for the past ten years and they were going to lose it. Silas tried to help keep that from happening."

"I noticed expenses for a trip there a year ago. Has he been there since?"

"No. But the family sends him pictures and they keep him updated."

Zack grunted. "Pictures. You can't get a good perspective from a few pictures."

"They also send videos of two of the most promising two-year-olds."

Zack shook his head. "This is a sinkhole, Jenny."

"It was your father's decision to invest in the ranch. Why are you discussing it with *me?*"

"Because you keep the books. You can see what's happening. The Rocky D is still making a profit, but that profit is down, too."

"We don't just do this for the money," she reminded him softly.

He approached the ranch's finances from another angle. "Dad still has a full staff when a lot of the other ranches have cut back."

"Our horses need the care we give them. I'd cut *my* salary before I let anyone go."

"Do you have say over that or does Dad?"

"We make joint decisions. If you were here, he'd give your opinion weight, too."

"I doubt that. I don't think he's going to give it any weight now. *You're* not giving it any weight."

Her finger came to her lips and she looked as if she were about to weigh her own words. His gaze targeted that finger and her lips. She had such a kissable mouth. With her hair long and loose on her shoulders, he was more tempted by her wholesome beauty than he ever believed he could be.

"If you were going to stay involved in the Rocky D, everything would be different," she returned quietly.

"Stay involved from long distance or close up?" he asked, trying to see into her mind.

But she wasn't even giving him a glimpse. With another little shrug, she responded, "Either."

"You wouldn't want me looking over your shoulder." He was sure about that.

"It wouldn't be like that."

"Wouldn't it?"

The defiant look came into her brown eyes and she turned away and started to rise from the sofa.

He caught her arm. "We're not done."

"You're in my room, Zack, and if I ask you to leave—"

"You know I *would* leave. But I'd also be waiting for you in the morning to finish this."

"Finish what? We don't have anything to finish."

He waited a beat, let her think about the evening before. "Last night you told me the bare essentials. You've told me the minimum. There's obviously more. You couldn't hide the sadness in your eyes. So tell me about the miscarriage."

Slowly sitting on the sofa again, she lowered her gaze to her hands in her lap. "I can't. It still hurts."

"Jenny."

That bit of caring in his voice must have gotten to her because she finally raised her eyes to his. "Fifteen years ago when it happened, I thought it was over. I thought it was done. Your mom and dad both helped me concentrate on other things. They gave me more responsibility around here. Your mom practically let me take over the bookwork. Your dad gave me more horses to train and let me become involved in the PR of selling the ones we bred. Years passed and then your mom died, and all of it came rushing back."

Zack could feel his chest tighten with a years-old ache of his own.

"When you came home for your mom's funeral," she went on, her voice low, "I thought about telling you then. But you were hurting so much, why make you hurt more? Now, most days, I think I've forgotten about the miscarriage. I think I've moved on. But then I see a child with her mom. I spend time with Celeste and Clay and Abby. I teach kids how to ride. All the while I know that I'm getting older, and I wonder if I'll ever have another chance at motherhood. Maybe it will be better now that you know. But I don't think so. Because last night when I told you, I saw a change in *your* eyes, too."

The emotion in her voice drew him closer to her. He couldn't help sliding his arm around her.

She resisted at first, but then she relaxed against him and he held her.

They sat there a long time, watching the flames in the fireplace, feeling but not talking.

The warmth of Jenny's body seeped into Zack, heating up the cold chambers of his heart. The change felt odd and uncomfortable and unnerving. He'd distanced himself from his emotions for so long, it was hard to process what he was feeling. But there was one sensation that was familiar and easier than all the others.

He slid a hand under Jenny's hair and turned her face up to his. He didn't have to say a word because he found a response in her eyes that matched the desire she'd always ignited in him. He bent his head, giving her time to move away, stopping for just a moment to let his breath mingle with hers. When she closed her eyes, he knew she was giving in to an attraction that had started so many years ago.

He began the kiss slowly, with just the coaxing taste of what passion could be. After all, he'd learned finesse since they were teenagers. He'd learned what women liked. But then Jenny gave a soft sigh, opened her mouth and everything he thought he knew vanished. This kiss wasn't about technique or titillation. It was about raw feelings they'd once shared and a hunger that still remained. He knew he shouldn't kiss her. He did know that. But Jenny was old memories, old feelings, feelings he hadn't experienced after he'd left her.

His thoughts shifted into such a high gear they were no more. Kissing Jenny was all that seemed to matter. The desire he felt was so startlingly strong, it drove him where he didn't want to go. They'd had something together. They'd lost something even greater. They'd lost a child. And now for a few moments, he had to try to get something back.

She seemed just as eager to try. Her hands were at the back of his neck...in his hair. She gave a little moan that he remembered all too well. Heat poured from him into her and back again that had nothing to do with that fire in the room. That was a fake fire anyhow. What was happening between them was *real.*

Jenny's body was soft against his. His fingers went to the tiny buttons on her gown as his tongue searched her mouth. He felt like a fumbling idiot when he couldn't open them fast enough. He was experienced at this. He should be doing a quicker job...a better job. Finally, he'd undone a quarter of the buttons and he could slip his hand inside her gown. He felt her start and wondered why. After all, she was thirty-three. She must have had partners, a few at least. It was no secret that men found her beautiful.

Yet she'd been a virgin when they'd had sex the first time...the only time. It shouldn't have happened. He'd intended to leave without going that far.

When his fingertips touched her breast, his hunger for her shook him. She pressed into his hand and rubbed against his palm. He wanted their clothes off. He didn't even care if they made it to the bed. The floor would do. His mouth twisted over hers and angled until his tongue explored deeper. It seemed to matter that he possess her.

Suddenly, everything stopped. Jenny tore away, pulled her nightgown closed and looked at him as if he were a stranger.

"No," she said on a sob. "This can't happen. I won't *let* it happen."

"Jenny." He reached for her trying to draw her to him again.

But she leaned away. "What do you think you're doing, Zack?"

The question swam around his head until he realized he couldn't answer it with any kind of logical response. Finally he admitted, "I'm not sure." His own voice was too husky, too filled with emotions he didn't want to acknowledge.

Where she had looked angry and almost defiant before, now her expression softened.

He reached out and took her hand, just held it in silence for a few moments. "We're still attracted to each other."

"That doesn't matter," she said quickly. "We know there's nowhere to go. Maybe I should have told you about the baby so many years ago. But I didn't want to hurt you then and I didn't mean to hurt you now."

Had he kissed her because he didn't know where to go with the feelings the loss had caused? Because the fact that they'd lost a child hurt too much to express in words? Finding out about the baby had cracked the shell he'd built around his heart. Cracked it, but not broken it. He knew better than to open up his heart again, especially to Jenny. She was so sure there was no world outside of the Rocky D. She was so sure that security was so much more important than dreams. There was no such thing as security and all anyone ever had were dreams.

"I didn't know how to react," he confessed. "I guess we both just got caught up in...the moment." Actually, he was embarrassed he hadn't been the one to stop it. He was dismayed that the same thing could have happened tonight that had happened in the hayloft on their graduation night. No, it wouldn't be the same at all. Now he carried a condom.

"What are you thinking?" she asked quietly.

"Nothing important."

"Your face went all dark. Your eyes changed."

"Don't try to read me like one of your horses."

With a sigh, she buttoned her nightgown. "I didn't want you in my room for a good reason."

"Then you shouldn't have run away from me all afternoon and evening."

She looped her hair over one ear. "You won't be home for that long, Zack. This shouldn't be so hard."

"This isn't hard. The fact that you didn't trust me enough to tell me about the baby before now is hard. The fact that my parents kept it from me is hard. What you've been through had to have been unimaginably hard."

His understanding brought vulnerability back to her face, and he realized now he'd taken advantage of that vulnerability, something he'd never done with a woman before. The women that he dated on the west coast knew the score. He chose women who didn't want entanglements any more than he did.

His personal life was a train rushing nowhere. Had he dated Rachel because he'd been bored? Restless? Searching for something he couldn't find? Had he dated Rachel because she was the extreme opposite of Jenny? Was that a pattern with him?

He swore and rose to his feet. "I should have gone outside and made some headway with Dusty. I didn't mean to...turn my sense of loss back at you."

All buttoned up now, she stood, too. To his surprise, she took a step closer and lightly touched his jaw. "We could have just talked, Zack, about what you felt and about what I felt. You express yourself so well in films, but you have such a tough time in person."

Wasn't that just the crux of it? Jenny had always seen too much. He didn't like the fact that she seemed to see through to his soul now.

He was the one who moved away this time. He crossed to her door, opened it and left her room. When the door shut with a click, he wondered just how soon he could return to California—because his staying here at the Rocky D wasn't good for him or his dad or Jenny.

Chapter Seven

With a sideways glance so his father wouldn't know he was watching him, Zack took a quick assessing look at Silas as they walked down the uneven stony path from the house to the barn. Zack suggested easily, "Maybe you should have brought your cane."

His dad scowled at him. "Don't even suggest it. I'm not an invalid. It's bad enough I have to take all that medication."

They walked in silence until they crossed the road and ambled up the loose gravel to the side door of the barn.

Once inside, Zack asked, "How do you feel?" This was his father's first sojourn to the outbuildings.

"I'm fine."

Zack had known his dad would say that, but he looked a bit winded. "The equipment for the exercise room is being delivered this afternoon. A nurse will be coming tomorrow. My guess is, she'll start you on the treadmill."

"I wonder what people do who can't afford an exercise room and a nurse," his father grumbled.

"You could be going into Flagstaff."

"That's a trek. Maybe I should donate enough money to build a cardiac rehab center at the urgent care place in town."

At first, Zack didn't think his father was serious, but as he studied his face, he saw that he was. "You'd consider that?"

"I'd consider giving a chunk and letting somebody start a fund drive. It's not as if when I die, you're going to need the money."

"No, I won't, but Jenny might. Have you included her in your will?"

"Do you think that's something you deserve to know?"

"I'm just asking. If you don't want to tell me, that's fine."

"Stop being so damn diplomatic," his father ordered with some of his old fire. "You've been treating me like a favorite uncle who's suddenly on his deathbed. I know that's not how you feel. Don't you think honesty between us would go a lot further?"

"And what do you want me to be honest about?" Zack asked, bracing himself for the inevitable.

"For starters, how angry you are you had to come back here in the first place. I know you don't want to be here."

As Zack remained silent, his father weighed his expression.

"You don't, do you?"

"No, I don't," Zack admitted. "But...this time being back here, remembering Mom being here, feels good in some ways."

Silas thought about that. "I think about her over the holidays most of all." Silas stopped at Hercules's stall and rubbed the horse's nose. The gelding snuffled and nuzzled Silas's hand as if he'd missed him.

"You know, Dad, you're going to have to make better investments than that horse farm in Kentucky if you want money to give to charity *or* money to leave to Jenny."

"I didn't buy in to that farm for an investment."

"You expected it to *lose* money?"

"*Expected* isn't the right word. I'm just not surprised. You know, not everything's about winning or making money."

"Since when is that your philosophy?"

His father didn't bristle at the comment. "Maybe the past few years. You should see those thoroughbreds, Zack. Their beauty is a gift to this earth."

His father never used to talk like this. He never thought about charity or doing something for his fellow man. Could Jenny be right? Was his father changing?

"And when do you think you're going to see those thoroughbreds again?"

"When I'm feeling better than I am now."

Zack glanced over the horses in the everyday barn, thought about the other barns, the foals up to the two-year-olds. "You have beautiful horses here, Dad. Why isn't that enough?"

"Why do you keep making movies?"

"You think there's a connection?"

"If you think about it long enough, you'll find the connection. It's about *more* and *what is* and experiencing every little thing while you can. Big things, too. Did you and Jenny have a talk?"

Understanding the leap in his father's thought processes from what was important to precious moments, he said, "We talked. She told me about her miscarriage. You don't have to worry about keeping the secret any longer."

"So you're mad at me for that, *too*." Silas exhaled with a sigh.

"I don't know. I'm still trying to take it all in. One moment I hear she was pregnant, the next she tells me she lost the baby. Do you think she did it on purpose?" That had been the question rolling around most in Zack's mind.

But at that inquiry, his father turned away from the horses and looked squarely at him. "You *know* Jenny. How could you even think that?"

"She was young and scared and didn't know what to do. That's how I could think it."

His father was already shaking his head. "Jenny has more guts than that. I do think, like most teenagers, she might have believed she was invincible. She thought she could ride and train and everything would be okay. But she had too much on her mind, got distracted, lost control of the horse for just a minute. That's all it took. Afterward, she was so sad I didn't know if she'd come out of it. Your mom stayed with her, talked to her, sat with her, made her eat and finally she started to heal."

Silas capped Zack's shoulder. "If you're half the man

I think you are, you're going to need to grieve, too. It's like it happened when she told you, right?"

Zack knew now that last night with Jenny, the sexual storm that had driven him, had been about grief and reclaiming life. But he hadn't confided in his father in much longer than fifteen years, so it wasn't something he could do easily now.

Stuffing the turmoil he felt about Jenny and the miscarriage, he gave a shrug. "I'll deal with it." In the next breath, he asked, "Are you ready to go back in?"

Silas shook his head and muttered, "You really are your father's son. Whether you like it or not, Zack, you're a lot like me. But you don't have to make the same mistakes I made."

Zack wasn't going to ask his dad to elaborate on the similarities between them. He concentrated on the differences...because that was a lot easier.

Snow had started falling again the night before. After Michael and Tanya's lesson on Saturday, Zack asked Michael what he'd like to shoot. The eleven-year-old announced he'd like to make snow angels with his sister. If Zack would help, they could videotape each other.

Zack checked the settings on the camcorder, remembering his own when he was in high school. He was used to much more sophisticated equipment now but this would get the job done for Michael and Tanya. He didn't know where Jenny had disappeared to but maybe she just didn't want to be out here doing this with him. He really did understand. If they got within a foot of each other, they'd melt the snow all around them.

Michael took hold of the camcorder to tape his sister.

He told her, "Say hi to Mom and Dad and wish them a Merry Christmas."

Tanya obeyed with a happy smile and a wave, then she lay down in the snow to make her angel.

Zack hefted Michael up onto his shoulder.

"Shoot it from up there. You'll get a better angle."

"Looks great!" Michael said as he let the tape run. He started humming "Jingle Bells" as he taped Tanya and that gave Zack an idea. When Tanya's turn came, Zack lifted her up onto his shoulder so she could do the same thing.

Suddenly, Jenny came around the corner from the barn. She stopped short when she saw Zack with Tanya on his shoulder. He could imagine what she was thinking. A child of theirs would be fourteen now, would be learning his talents, or her abilities, would be becoming an independent person, might be rebelling against parental authority.

Zack caught a glimpse of what Jenny was pulling behind her and felt as if someone had kicked him in the gut. It was the oddest sensation. She was pulling the sled he'd used when he was a boy. His father had bought it for him when he was seven and his mother had warned him too many times to count that he should be careful. Of course he hadn't been and she'd had to bandage him up. But he and his dad had taken that sled to the highest hills on the property. His father had approved of Zack's flying over hillocks and around brush, only to trudge up to the top of the hill again and start all over. Where had those memories been hiding all these years?

But Jenny couldn't know about that, could she?

When Tanya finished taping, he swung her down to the ground. She ran over to Michael and tried to hold the camera steady as he wrote "Merry Christmas" in the snow.

Pulling the sled, Jenny stopped beside Zack. "Look what I found."

"Where did you find it?" Zack asked, his voice huskier than he'd like it to be.

"It was in the storage barn behind some old tools. I'd seen it there when I was looking for Silas's toolbox. I thought the kids would like to use it in their video." She studied Zack thoughtfully. "Should I have not brought it out?"

"No, it's fine. In fact, it will be perfect."

Snow had begun falling again. Jenny wore a red knit cap, a crimson scarf around her neck and a yellow down jacket. Snowflakes settled on her bangs and eyelashes and Zack suddenly wished he had a camera in his hand to take a video of *her*.

"Come on," he encouraged her. "Let's get this done before their mom arrives. We wouldn't want to spoil the surprise."

He turned away before she could see too much on his face, too much he was trying to hide yet couldn't.

First Michael pulled Tanya on the sled, singing "Joy to the World" and waving. Then Tanya tried to pull Michael but had a tough time of it even though she was a good sport. Zack knew the recorder was taping their laughter as well as their Christmas carols and the fun they were having. That laughter would be the best present they could give their parents.

Jenny suggested, "Now both of you get in the sled. I'll pull it while Zack shoots."

Zack framed the moving picture, Jenny pulling the

two children in the sled. She would make a terrific mother. He felt the hard hand of fate squeeze his heart.

He called to them, "We'd better call it a wrap, or your mom's going to catch us doing this."

The kids tumbled from the sled and ran over to Zack.

Michael beamed up at him. "Thank you so much for helping us do this."

Zack had reviewed some of the footage on the camera. "You did really well, both of you. Now I have a question for you. If I can find a machine that will transfer your video onto a DVD, are you interested?"

"Really, you can do that?" Michael asked enthusiastically.

"Sure. I can even put a beginning and end on it like a movie. Would you like that?"

Both kids were jumping up and down now. "That would be great," Michael enthused. "We have a DVD player. We'd still have the tape, right?"

"Right. You'd have both. Your parents might like that."

"Thanks so much, Mr. Decker," Michael said, giving him a huge hug. "You're going to make our Christmas super."

Tanya was a little more sedate about her thanks, but she gave him a hug, too. Zack couldn't remember when he'd last been hugged like that by kids. His heart seemed to warm up and grow and forget about everything that wasn't good and innocent and carefree.

"I'll take the sled back to the barn," Jenny said.

"Better stow the camera in your backpack," Zack reminded Michael.

Before he did, Michael removed the tape and handed it to Zack.

They had just reached the arena when Michael and Tanya's mother drove her truck onto the gravel. The two children went to join her. She waved, watched them climb into the truck, then took off.

Zack turned the tape around in his hand. What more could parents want than memories of their children in living color?

Staring down at the tape, Zack didn't hear Jenny when she came up beside him, but he did feel her hand when she placed it on his jacket and squeezed his arm. "What are you thinking?"

"I'm thinking losing a child isn't a pain that goes away easily."

"Oh, Zack." She stepped into his embrace, letting him hold her again because he was the one person who understood better than anyone.

They gave comfort to each other, oblivious to the snow landing on their noses and settling on their cheeks. When Jenny looked up at him, he saw the tears and he knew her telling him had opened the old wound wide. He hugged her again and she snuggled into his shoulder. She fit there so perfectly.

"Kiss me, Jenny."

"Do you think the pain will go away if I do?"

"No. I tried that last night. It didn't work. But when you do kiss me, I forget about everything else for a little while."

"So do I," she admitted, lifting her mouth to his.

He didn't mean to deepen the kiss. He didn't mean to coax every ounce of life out of it. He didn't mean for the world to fall away until only the two of them stood there. But that's what happened.

He broke the kiss, leaning away to look at her. "Attraction's hard to deny."

"But we're both trying to, and we have to. Maybe it will be easier this week with Thanksgiving and all. I want Silas to know he's loved and cared about. So I'm asking Mikala and her aunt Anna to join us. They really have nowhere to go for the holiday, either. We can celebrate together and maybe Silas can see he still has a lot of years to go. That can be meaningful."

"Are you going to have help other than Martha for this dinner party?"

"No. Mikala said she'd help."

"So you want an old-fashioned Thanksgiving?"

"Yes, I do. Don't you?"

"Holidays don't mean much to me anymore, Jenny."

"You don't go anywhere special for Thanksgiving or Christmas?"

"I might not even be home over a holiday. I'd rather be shooting a film somewhere. I don't see holidays the way Mom did, the way you do."

"Holidays should be a time to spend with family and friends, to appreciate the reasons you're together."

He frowned when he realized that's exactly what she truly believed. "I think you've read too many greeting cards."

"It's the way I feel, Zack. It has nothing to do with greeting cards, or what the commercial world is trying to sell me. It's about the feeling I have in here—" she tapped her chest "—when I'm with people I know care about me."

"We have such different views of life," he said.

"They don't have to be so different. Promise me something."

"What?" he asked warily.

"That at the end of Thanksgiving Day, we'll talk about this again."

"You're serious."

"Yes, I am. Is it a promise?"

Looking into Jenny's coffee-brown eyes, reading the pleasure she got from standing out here in the snow with him, talking about things that mattered to her, he said, "I promise."

But as soon as he said it, he wished he hadn't. He didn't make promises anymore. They were too easy to break. But with this one, he had a feeling Jenny wouldn't let him break it.

What kind of holiday would Thanksgiving Day be?

On Thanksgiving Day, Jenny trimmed holly leaves from a branch, washed them and used them as decoration on a large fruit tart. The delicious aroma of roasting turkey filled the kitchen. She hadn't seen Zack all morning. He had a habit of closeting himself in his office when he didn't want to deal with her or his father. Of course, she hadn't searched him out, either. Being with Zack was too exciting, too painful, too regret-filled.

Martha checked the cooking potatoes one last time and said, "I'm going to make sure the dining room is ready," then left Jenny alone in the kitchen.

Not long after, Zack strode in. "Everything smells wonderful," he said. "Dad wants to know if he gets a free pass for today."

"Not exactly a free pass. We won't be using cream in the whipped potatoes. The turkey's good for him and I made apple stuffing instead of the usual sausage. We're good to go." As Zack approached her, the heat level in the kitchen seemed to go up a few degrees.

"And what about the desserts?" he asked with a quirked brow, as if normal conversation was all they needed between them, as if normal conversation could solve everything.

"Martha made a low-fat, low-sugar pumpkin pie, and the fruit tart has a whole wheat crust. He can have a sliver of each."

Beside her now, Zack checked her handiwork. "Did you do this yourself?"

"I did."

Slowly, Zack reached toward her, his thumb brushing her upper lip. "I think somebody was tasting the fruit."

She laughed self-consciously, because his touch made her tremble all over. "You caught me. Strawberries."

The simmering desire in his blue eyes told her he wanted to do more than touch her. He wanted to kiss her again. But he wouldn't, and she wouldn't let him. She had to do everything in her power to stay away from him.

The timer went off on the stove. "That's for the turkey," she said a bit shakily.

"Do you want me to get it out?"

"That would be a help. Martha and I wrestled it into the oven, but we certainly wouldn't want to drop it now."

Zack chuckled as he went to the oven, opened it, then took the oven mitts from the counter. He lifted the pan so easily, Jenny wondered how much he worked out in L.A. He'd always been all muscle, with broad shoulders and a lean torso. The past fifteen years hadn't changed that. It hadn't changed a lot of things. He was wearing a snap-button shirt today and black jeans, just like he used to. His boots were ever-present now.

She'd dressed carefully, telling herself she wanted to be festive for their company. She'd worn the pearl earrings Olivia had given her. In her turquoise sweater and skirt and suede high-heeled boots, she felt festive and put-together. After all, today was Thanksgiving. She'd felt like dressing up.

She'd thought about all the times her father had missed holidays with her. Would he even call today? She couldn't expect him to. And without the expectation, she wouldn't be disappointed.

"Did you get much work done?" she asked Zack as he took the lid off the turkey and took a whiff in appreciation.

"I wasn't working, at least not in the office. I was out there with Dusty. He actually took a piece of apple from my hand."

"Oh, Zack, that's wonderful! Did he run afterward?"

"Of course. He wasn't going to wait around to see if I wanted it back."

She laughed. "You're making such progress with him. I just hope when you leave—"

"He's not as skittish with you anymore, either. Is there anything else you need me to do?" Zack asked, looking around the kitchen, unwilling to address the subject of his leaving.

"Not right now. Everything else is last minute. As soon as I see Mikala's car in the drive—she's bringing veggie casseroles—I'll put the water on for tea." When Zack would have turned to go, she asked him, "If you were in L.A., what *would* you be doing?"

He shrugged. "That's hard to say. I might have been alone, walking the beach, taking advantage of the day off, or I might have spent it working on script notes for my next project. Or I might have gone north for some skiing. Why?"

"I just wondered. Most of the things you mentioned, you would have been doing alone, except for the skiing if you took someone along."

"Did you ever ski?" he asked her.

She shook her head, wondering if he was thinking again how limited her life experiences were.

"You should try it. It's great exercise. But for the most part, it's a solitary sport."

"You wouldn't have taken someone along?"

"Not if I wanted to ski."

Jenny realized exactly what *that* meant. Zack was a focused person. If he went to the mountains to enjoy the outdoors and to ski, that's what he'd do. If on the other hand, he went to the mountains to hook up with someone in a cozy little cabin and have sex, that's what he'd do.

The kiss in her bedroom played in her mind all over again and she felt her face getting hot. "I'd better see to the potatoes," she told him, going to the stove and cutting off their conversation. But Zack couldn't be shut down that easily. He came up behind her and turned her around to face him.

"There's nothing wrong with the way I live my life or the way you live yours. They're just different lifestyles."

Were they so different? He walled people out and kept them at a distance. Because he'd gotten hurt too many times in the past? Because she'd been one of those reasons he'd put up walls? She let people in, but not men, at least not men who wanted a relationship. Because she was afraid they'd let her down...as her father had always done? Because she was afraid they'd leave... as Zack had done?

She said the truth running around in her head. "I think your life is lonely, Zack, and maybe mine is limited."

Just then, the three-tone chime on the front door echoed through the entire house. They'd been too engrossed in each other to hear a car driving up outside. If they became engrossed in each other again, would their walls come tumbling down? Or would they simply be opening themselves to more heartache?

Chapter Eight

Jenny loved holidays, especially when they were like this one, with friends and people she cared about sitting around the dining room table. She'd dreamed of a Thanksgiving like this when she was a child. Now it was a reality.

Yet, sometimes she felt as if she were living someone else's life. This wasn't her house. These weren't her horses. Silas wasn't her father. Really if she got down to it, she was an employee on the ranch, just like Hank and Tate and Ben and the other workers.

Still, when her gaze met Zack's she felt a sense of... belonging. How crazy was that? She didn't belong with Zack. They were way too different...and five hundred miles apart. As she passed the green beans to Mikala, she noticed Mikala watching Silas and Anna. They hadn't stopped talking since Anna arrived and Silas looked more animated than he had since his procedure.

"They're getting along well," Jenny said in a low voice.

"I think they dated once upon a time," Mikala said.

"What happened?"

"Aunt Anna has never told me much. I mean, I always knew she and Silas went to school together. But he worked so hard trying to give the Rocky D a good reputation. He was always on a horse, in the barn, going to sales, traveling to other ranches meeting clients. So I think his ambition got in the way. Then he met Olivia Reynolds. Aunt Anna told me she'd never really had a chance after that."

"Look at them now. Even your aunt seems to be... sparkling."

"Hmm," Mikala said, noncommittally. "Zack doesn't look as if he's happy about it."

As Jenny watched Zack, she had to wonder what he was thinking...what he was feeling. She'd lost her mom, too, and missed her desperately. No one could ever, *ever* take a mom's place. Yet, as she'd grown older and her father had been away more and more, she'd wondered if he'd met the right woman, if they could have formed a family. The thing was, he never had, or at least he'd never brought anyone home.

Zack's experience, on the other hand, had been altogether different. He'd known his mother into adulthood, and the sun had risen and set with her. His father had been the bad guy, the disapproving distant dad who had done his mother wrong. Now she wondered if Zack would resent seeing his father happy, or if he just didn't want to see a woman fill his mother's place.

Mikala engaged Zack in conversation. When Jenny tried to do the same and their gazes met, she couldn't seem to find any words. At one point, when they all seemed to be finished with the main course, Silas focused his attention on Jenny.

"What do you think about having dessert in the living room?"

This was a departure from their usual routine, but Jenny liked the idea. "Sure, we can do that." She wondered if Silas thought his guests would stay longer if they were comfortable.

Silas rose to his feet. "Wonderful! Coffee and dessert in the living room, and maybe Anna and I can share some of the legends circulating around Miners Bluff from when we were kids."

"The Preservation Society is trying to gather them all," Anna explained. "Celeste Sullivan is helping us put them all together in a book."

"Celeste is also working on a book with Clay's mom about the Sullivan family history, isn't she?" Jenny asked.

"She is. And I understand even Harold is contributing his time. Celeste's marriage to Clay has brought that family together. It's wonderful to see."

"I suppose a good marriage can do that," Jenny responded with a quick glance at Zack.

His expression was so blank she knew he was really working at keeping it that way. He'd once told her that after seeing his parents' arguments, he would never marry. Maybe that was the real reason why she hadn't gone with him to L.A. Maybe because she'd wanted to believe in the power of marriage—and wanted to be with a man who believed in it, too.

Over coffee, fruit tart and pumpkin pie, Anna and Silas told some of the legends of Miners Bluff. Zack appeared totally engrossed. He'd obviously never heard them from his father before. They were stories about the miners who worked the first copper mine, tales about the drums some visitors heard when they were exploring Feather Peak. Jenny wondered if Zack was seeing his dad in a new light, but was almost afraid to hope.

After Anna and Mikala left, Silas gave Jenny a hug. "I'm grateful you made this Thanksgiving special." He looked at Zack. "And I'm glad you're here." Then turning away from both of them, he said, "I'm tired. I'm going to my room and fall asleep in front of the TV."

Once Silas had turned away, Zack stared after him.

"He and Anna seemed to get along well." Jenny thought she'd just throw the comment out there and see what was going on in Zack's head.

"What are you suggesting?"

"That hinting to your dad that he might want to go on a date with Anna could be a good idea."

"Jenny..." Zack's tone was filled with warning.

"What? It's not so far-fetched. Dating Anna could give Silas some of his old verve back."

"Verve? Look what he did to my mother!"

"Can't you see the man he is now?"

Zack raked his hand through his hair and she realized it would probably take a lot more than a few weeks for him to see how much Silas had changed.

She knew she should keep her mouth shut, turn away and go to her suite. But she couldn't. "You know, Zack, your dad made bad decisions, but your mother did, too. She stayed with him instead of holding him accountable for his actions. I think she liked her life here, and she didn't want it to change. She's the one who got into that small plane, knowing full well the weather could be bad. You're blaming him for the decision *she* made that night. Is that fair?"

"I thought you loved my mother," Zack said, accusation written all over his face.

"I did. I do. And I love your dad. That doesn't make me blind. That just makes it even more important that I accept who they were and who they are. It takes two people to fight, two people not to resolve the problems in their marriage."

The house phone rang breaking the dense silence between her and Zack. "I'll get it," Jenny said, "in case Martha already went to her quarters." Checking the caller ID, she murmured, "It might be my dad."

Her heart lifted at the thought.

"Go ahead and take it. I'm going out to take Dusty a Thanksgiving treat. Hank, Tate and Ben should be back, but I'll check the bunkhouse to make sure."

With a nod, he left her in the foyer.

Phone in hand, seeing the caller ID said OUT OF AREA, she answered, "Hello?"

"Hey, baby. Happy Thanksgiving!"

Hearing her father's voice always created a mixed rush of feelings. She kept telling herself it didn't matter if he called. She no longer waited for calls or visits. Yet when she heard his deep baritone, she remembered the times he'd hoisted her on his shoulders, took her to the rodeo to watch the horses, looked at her mother as if she'd been the most important person in his world. Now she felt…relieved that his latest job of teaching techniques to rodeo clowns and cowboys hadn't gotten him injured. "Thanks. What are you doing?"

"I'm here at a restaurant with some of my rodeo buddies—great turkey and pie—just outside of San Antonio. You ought to come down here sometime. You'd like the Riverwalk."

She'd read about the Riverwalk and its shops and boutiques and restaurants. Her dad just didn't understand that the traveling bug had never bit her, probably because he'd always been gone so much that he didn't realize she saw traveling as a way to escape responsibility. Because of the life her dad had led, she'd always wanted to put down roots, to dig in her heels, to make a life that was sturdy and safe.

"How long are you going to be in San Antonio?" She couldn't stop herself from asking. "Do you think you can get back to Miners Bluff for the holidays? It would be great to spend Christmas together." As always, she issued the invitation without getting her hopes up.

"I don't think so, darlin'. I'm going to be one of the teachers at a training camp between Christmas and New Year's. The money's too good to turn down."

At her silence, he went on, "You'll have a big ole Christmas tree at Silas Decker's place, and probably any present you could ask for. You don't need me mucking around."

Maybe her father had just never understood how much she needed him. "Silas had a heart attack, Dad. He's recovering now, but I'm not exactly sure what we'll be doing for Christmas. Zack came home while he was in the hospital and he's staying a few weeks."

"Zack, huh? How do you feel about that, having him there again?"

Her father had known she'd been smitten with Zack. She hadn't been able to hide it. But he hadn't known about the pregnancy or the miscarriage, or how broken-hearted she'd been when Zack had left. "This is a big place. We run into each other now and then."

He laughed. "Oh, I bet you do. Does he act all high and mighty like he's better than everybody else? That's the way those celebrity types are."

As she thought over exactly how Zack did act, she found herself thinking that it wasn't like a celebrity. "No, he's not like that. He's more introspective, more cynical, more...alone."

"That's hard to believe. Hey, maybe I should ask him to back my idea for starting up a clown camp."

"Oh, Dad, you wouldn't."

"Why not? He could be part investor."

"Everybody wants something from him. I think that's partially why he is the way he is. So don't even think about asking him for money."

There was a very long pause, then her father said, "I understand."

She was glad he understood at least. He'd never really understood her. Ever since her mother died, she'd had no one to depend on. When she tried to depend on her dad, he'd let her down, not once but over and over and over again. Her life just wasn't important enough to him to be part of it. Yet she could never close the door.

"I wish you could come back for Christmas," she said, trying to keep the wistfulness from her voice. "You know if you change your mind, you're welcome."

"You know I wouldn't be comfortable staying there."

"You could always stay in the bunkhouse. I don't think Hank, Tate and Ben would mind."

"We'll see, darlin'."

Jenny swallowed hard, then blurted out, "Why don't

you want to get close to me, Dad? You never have. I always thought something was wrong with me."

"Jenny, no! There's nothing wrong with *you*. You're beautiful and smart. You always have been." He stopped, maybe trying to rearrange his thoughts, and she gave him the time. Finally he admitted, "You look like your momma. Even when you were a little girl, you did. After she died, I couldn't look at you without seeing her. It hurt. If I'd stayed home with you, I would have drunk myself into an early grave."

She didn't know why she'd brought this up. Because Zack's return had stirred the pot?

"What about now?"

After a few beats of silence, her dad sighed. "Aw, Jenny. When you love someone and you lose them, the pain never goes away. It comes back in a wave when you least expect it."

"Can't you just appreciate the ways I'm like Mom, but also know the ways we're different? Can't you separate us? Can't we just be a daughter and a dad getting to know each other?"

"That was a mouthful."

"No, it was a heartful." She waited a beat and added, "Silas is great, and he does act like a father. But he's *not* my father. *You* are."

"Jenny, life is what it is. People are who they are. You're old enough to accept the fact that I'm a wanderer. I don't stay in one place. You do."

After a long pause, he said, "I've got to go."

"All right, Dad. Thanks for the call."

"You take care, you hear?"

Before she could even say "I love you, Dad," he was gone.

* * *

Jenny wasn't sure why she went to the exercise room later that night. Usually when she couldn't sleep, she went to the barn, or at least outside on the balcony that overlooked the rose garden. There she could remember happier times with Olivia. She could remember strolling with Zack in and out of the paths, stealing kisses under the arbor. But tonight, she thought Silas's new elliptical trainer might be what she needed. Maybe she could work off steam, calories and exhaust herself so that when she fell into bed, she'd go to sleep.

Her dad's phone calls always troubled her, and this one was no exception. When she was a kid, she'd watched out the window, waiting for him to come home. She'd waited for phone calls that had never come. She'd longed for daddy-hugs at bedtime when he was gone. As a teenager, she'd gotten used to being disappointed by him. She'd sloughed off his absences and just pretended they didn't matter. But the truth was, when he'd so readily agreed to the Deckers taking her in during her senior year, she'd just felt unwanted.

You're an adult now, she told herself. *Get over it.* Isn't that what she expected Zack to do?

She heard the hum of the treadmill before she reached the exercise room. Silas certainly wouldn't be in here this time of night, not without someone to watch over him. So it must be—

As she stood in the doorway, Zack was unaware of her presence. He was shirtless with a towel slung around his neck. He was jogging on the treadmill and she couldn't help but stare at the straightness of his spine, the smooth motion of his hips, his powerful thighs as he ran the difficult course he'd selected. Zack would never take an easy course. He would challenge himself with the hardest one.

His black hair was mussed as if he'd rubbed the towel over it. He stared ahead at the TV screen on the wall—the sound was turned down low and she didn't know how he could even hear it. But then she supposed he might just be reading the crawl across the bottom of the news channel. She knew she didn't make a sound when she entered. Her athletic shoes were silent on the wood floor. Still, he glanced over his shoulder spotting her. He appeared surprised, slowed his pace to a fast walk, then switched off the machine.

"I didn't mean to interrupt your workout."

He stepped off the treadmill and ran the towel over his face and down his chest. She couldn't look away. He'd had broad shoulders as a teenager, but now they were even broader. His chest was wider, covered with black hair tapering to a spot below his navel. The drawstring of his shorts kept her transfixed.

"I'm finished."

As her gaze traveled back up his torso to his eyes, her breath caught at the sheer virility emanating from him. Being in the same room with him had always affected her. But now, being in the same room with him looking so primal made her pulse quicken and her breath come in short puffs.

"Did you come in to work out?" he asked her, noticing her attire. She'd worn leggings and a tank with her hair in a topknot.

She motioned to the elliptical trainer. "I thought I'd try that out. I'd firm up different muscles than I use when riding."

He gave her a quick once-over. "I think you're firmed up just fine."

She felt the heat of the blush.

He grinned at her. "Aren't you used to compliments?"

"Not that kind," she admitted.

He shook his head. "I think you're running with the wrong crowd of men."

"I don't run with a crowd of men." And the implication was there—*like you do with women.*

His grin faded. "I know you don't. That was a stupid thing to say."

Admitting he'd made a mistake was something she didn't expect from Zack. Flustered, she searched for something substantial to hold on to, something that would distract her from the chemistry between them, the sexual vibrations beating along with her heart as loud as a primitive drum.

"Anna and I were discussing something I thought you might want to help with this year."

"Oh, yeah. What's that?" he asked warily.

"It's not another committee. Actually, we could really use another pair of hands."

She accompanied her words with a glance at his shoulders and arms and now he shifted as if he might be uncomfortable with her appraising him. Wasn't he used to women staring at him?

"I'm almost afraid to ask."

"Next Friday, we're meeting at the social hall at the firehouse to fill holiday baskets for needy families, and then we'll be delivering them. Do you think that's something you could help us with?"

When he was nonresponsive for a few seconds, she assumed he wanted to say no. "That's okay," she said, "I just thought I'd ask." She moved to the elliptical trainer and began to study the settings.

He moved quickly and was there beside her before she could blink. "I didn't say no."

"But you want to."

"You're reading me wrong, Jenny. I'm just wondering how the people in the community will like me pushing in when I'm not an insider anymore."

"Are you kidding me? You could never be an outsider here."

"You mean because of my father's name?"

"No. Because of your reputation. My gosh, Zack, don't you believe the residents here would be honored to work beside you? They might ask for your autograph!"

"Not in Miners Bluff."

"I've seen women go up to Silas in the feed store and ask for an autographed picture of you."

Zack laughed out loud. "And what does he say to that request?"

"He usually tells them you're too busy to take time to sign photographs, that you're working on your next blockbuster. He's proud of you, Zack, and anyone can hear it in his voice. So don't think for a minute that you wouldn't be accepted here. You're Miners Bluff, born and bred, and that's all that matters."

In the silence that followed, his gaze held hers. No words passed between them, but a whole history did. Finally she found her voice again, and said, "It would mean a lot to Silas if you stayed until Christmas." She remembered she'd told him they'd talk about holidays again at the end of the day. "Didn't you enjoy being here today?"

She almost thought he wasn't going to answer. But then he said, "Even if I did, staying wasn't in my plans."

"I know. But can't you think about changing them?"

He reached out and laid his hand alongside her neck, his thumb rubbing her jaw. Although she knew she should move away from his touch, she couldn't.

"Do *you* want me to stay?"

If she said she did, she'd be in trouble. If she said she didn't, she might be in just as much trouble. Either way, her feelings were going to show. Could he see she wanted to be held in his arms? Could he sense the tingling awareness that tempted her to lift her lips to his? She could feel his body heat, was familiar with his scent, knew that he had a birthmark on his right upper thigh, and a scar on his right knee.

If he kissed her now, they'd end up on the floor, tearing each other's clothes off.

The chirp of Zack's cell phone was an unwanted distraction. She realized he'd hooked it to the control panel of the treadmill. He must have been expecting a call.

"Take it," she said breathlessly.

When he leaned in closer, she shook her head. "Take it, Zack."

After hesitating one more moment to decide whether he wanted to acquiesce to her wishes or kiss her anyway, he sighed, swung away from her, and grabbed the phone. He recognized the number on the screen and he put the phone to his ear.

"Hi, Grant. How did it go?"

Jenny unabashedly listened. After all, Zack was right there and he wasn't moving away, so it must not matter if she heard.

"I thought the terms were settled."

He listened for a while. "Damn it, Grant, this isn't a good time."

He listened again. "You're sure we can handle this in one more meeting?" Zack frowned. "Not a conference call or a video conference? All right, let me think about it. I'll get back to you tomorrow morning." He ended the call and laid the phone on the treadmill control panel once more.

"Problems?" she asked, curious.

"Complications." He studied her for a few very long moments.

"What?" she asked, unnerved by his intense concentration on her.

"You want me to stay until Christmas, so I'll make you a deal. If you fly to California with me for a few days, I'll stay until the holiday. What do you say? Will you go to L.A. with me?"

Fly to L.A. with him. He'd asked her to go with him once before and she'd refused. If she refused now—

"You have to go back now? Is it really necessary?" Or did he just want to get away from the Rocky D and Silas? Had he had enough?

"My next project is important to me because it's a departure from what I usually do. If I went for marketable again, funding wouldn't be a problem. But a documentary? I have to get one particular investor to sign on the dotted line. He's hesitant. I have to convince him by giving him my vision in person."

She could see how sincere he was. His work gave purpose to his life. But that still didn't explain the deal he was proposing.

"Why do you want me to go with you?"

He hesitated for a few moments, then admitted, "I want you to get a glimpse of my world."

Of what she'd missed by refusing him so long ago? Silas needed him to stay until Christmas. They seemed to be relating to each other and a few more weeks could strengthen new bonds between them. And, to be honest, she wanted more time with Zack, too. She couldn't refuse him this time.

Inhaling a deep breath, both excited and a little fearful of venturing out of her realm, she agreed. "Okay. I'll go with you to L.A. if you'll stay until the new year."

When he smiled and extended his hand, she let his fingers envelop hers. Then an idea hit her with some force. She'd be staying at Zack's house—alone with him.

This trip to L.A. could be the biggest adventure of her life.

Chapter Nine

The Saturday after Thanksgiving, Jenny studied Zack's house, part of an exclusive community near Malibu. Surrounded by coastal trees and shrubs, it was unique and surprisingly welcoming.

"What do you think?" Zack asked as she stepped into the entrance, wondering exactly why she'd come, why she'd left Silas, why the ground beneath her feet seemed to be shifting.

When she didn't answer right away, he came up beside her and put his hand on her shoulder. "Are you still worried about Dad?"

"No," she answered honestly. "We'll only be gone two nights. Martha said she'll stay within shouting distance and Hank promised to stop in often, too."

Jenny returned to studying the architecture of Zack's house. Its intriguing quality lured her deeper inside.

The stone-accented and wooden-beamed exterior led into a high-vaulted, A-framed ceiling with those same accents inside. It was an open plan and she could see beyond the living room to the sunroom, deck and ocean. Taking a few steps deeper inside, she spotted another set of sliding glass doors off the kitchen with its granite counters and stainless steel appliances, its dining area with a glass table and comfortable-looking blue and green fabric-covered chairs. The colors inside the house reflected the sea, accented by natural materials mirroring hues of the outside landscape. Zack had obviously added his own preferences—dark wood bookshelves with rows and rows of videotapes and DVDs, a group of framed photos depicting various scenes from movie sets, an oil painting of a rocky cliff reflecting shadowed moonlight.

The photos on the mantel were telling. There was one of his mother in the corral of the Rocky D, one of Dawson and Clay and Zack outside a sports arena, probably in L.A. There was also an older one of Zack and Clay and Dawson standing around his first car in the parking lot of Miners Bluff High School. Jenny remembered taking that photo herself with Zack's camera. Yet there were no pictures of Silas or of her.

Zack came up behind her and dropped her overnight case to the sunset-colored scatter rug.

"What do you think?" he asked again gruffly, so close to her, she could feel his body heat.

She wasn't exactly sure what he wanted her thoughts on. When she turned to face him, her heart thumped madly. "Your house is beautiful, Zack. It could be a retreat from the world." She gestured to the view of the ocean. "I can imagine you sitting here, peering out there, seeing scene after scene of a new movie flashing in your mind."

"That's exactly what I do. And the beach, for the most part, is private. My closest neighbors are away for months at a time."

A picture of the two of them on a private beach with no one around suddenly occupied her thoughts. Is that why she'd come? For intimacy with Zack? Or *had* she come to catch a glimpse of his lifestyle and find out whether he was simply the movie director and producer now, or still the boy she'd once known and loved?

She'd worn espadrilles to travel, along with jeans, a T-shirt and a windbreaker. He'd told her nights at the beach could be fifty degrees in late November. She'd been surprised that Zack had worn his boots instead of Italian loafers along with his jeans and a snap-button shirt. Was this the first time he'd brought something from the ranch here with him? Were his bitterness and resentment about the way he'd left the Rocky D fading away?

Standing there, gazing at each other, his blue eyes going darker, her own blood running faster, she might have asked him, but she didn't get the opportunity because his cell phone buzzed.

Grimacing, he took it from the holster on his belt. "I have to get this. It's about my meeting."

"I'll unpack," she said easily. "Just point me to the right room."

"Down the hall, second door on the left. Make yourself at home."

This didn't feel like home at all, because it was so different from what she knew. The ranch was dark paneling and leather, rawhide, suede and corduroy. Its rugs had Native American flair in jewel tones that were deep and dark and beautiful.

However, she *did* like the ocean.

Trailing the travel case behind her, she stopped in the kitchen and gazed out those sliding glass doors. To have the salt air and breeze and the beautiful colors right there was amazing. The sound of it must be, too. She couldn't wait to feel the sand between her toes. Yet, she felt a little strange in this house full of light and cream walls, glass and chrome and appliances that were shiny and new. She didn't know what to think about Zack and his life here, what he did to relax and what he did to connect.

From what she could tell, there was a master suite and two guest bedrooms. When she opened the second door on the left, she found a beautifully decorated room anyone would have felt at home in. There was a coral reef mural on one wall, a rich coral spread on the bed, a pale yellow carpet and distressed pale green furniture. When she opened the closet, she found it empty. Apparently, he didn't even need to store anything in it. It seemed Zack lived luxuriously but sparingly. Of course, he had a penthouse in town and a chalet in Vail. His life seemed unimaginable to her. Yet, when she watched him work with horses on the Rocky D, she knew he'd been denying a part of himself for a long time.

Forgetting about her suitcase, she crossed to the window. When she looked at the property next door— though next door was a relative term—it was a large estate and Jenny doubted whether neighbors borrowed a cup of sugar from each other around here.

She heard Zack coming down the hall, heard him

coming into the room, but she didn't turn around. Her Zack-radar knew when he was about a foot behind her.

"A different view from the one at the Rocky D," she murmured.

"We have roses here, too," he responded, his voice nonchalantly mellow.

Still, she didn't face him. "But you don't have four seasons. Do you see Christmas trees around here? I mean, do people have them in their homes?"

"Some do. You know, Jen, I didn't bring you out here to make comparisons." Something like impatience edged his tone. "I thought you might like to see beyond the boundaries of the Rocky D, beyond the boundaries of Miners Bluff. Open your eyes, Jen. There's a whole world out here."

She motioned to the estate outside, to the room, and the house beyond. "And what's in that world, Zack? I saw a few pictures out on the mantel, but nothing else that was really personal. Do you have many personal things at any one of the places where you live? Do you really *belong* anywhere?"

After a few beats of silence, he asked with a bit of exasperation, "Do you want to fight?"

Maybe she did want to rile him up. Maybe she wanted to make him feel. She took a deep breath and shook her head. "No, I don't want to fight. I just want to know where you really live. Which place do you call home? Which place reflects who you are? Which place makes you feel warm and cuddly and makes you feel as if you don't want to leave?"

His eyebrows arched. "Warm and cuddly? Did you ever know me to want warm and cuddly?"

She thought back to time spent in the barn when they'd cuddled in the straw.

He must have been revisiting the same memory because he muttered, "Scratch that. I'm not like you. I don't carry memories of my childhood with me to take out and look at. I don't hang on to possessions thinking they'll bring me good luck. I don't store things, hoping I'll use them one day."

"And why is that, Zack? Connections and bonds and dreams and memories are *not* bad things. I understand memories can bring pain, but they can bring happiness, too, even if it is a little nostalgic. When did you let go of needing roots? When did you stop having dreams?"

"My dreams are just different from yours. We're not the same. We never were."

"Except for one summer when we thought we belonged to each other," she refuted quietly.

She saw she'd hit home with that one. His eyes darkened and the corners of his lips turned down. She could see he was about to respond, maybe with a bit of temper, when his cell phone buzzed again.

She was sorry it had because she figuratively would have liked to have duked this one out.

He checked the screen, said, "Excuse me," and exited the bedroom.

While she heard the murmur of his voice down the hall, she started to unpack. A few minutes later, he reentered her room. "My driver will be here in about fifteen minutes to take you sightseeing. I have a meeting here this afternoon that will last a while."

"Does that mean I shouldn't come back until your meeting's over?"

His lips thinned. "Of course not. You can see as

much as you want to see, or as little. I thought you might like to go shopping on Rodeo Drive, see the stars' handprints at Grauman's Chinese. But if you prefer something quieter, and you just want to sit out on the deck and watch the ocean, that's fine, too."

She thought about it. "When Mikala came back from a conference out here, she told me about Olvera Street. She said the leather goods there are wonderful. And I'd like to visit the Getty Museum."

"Just tell my driver where you want to go. When the meeting's over, we can go out to a restaurant or have a picnic on the beach."

"I should think about that, too?"

"It's the only major decision you'll have to make while you're here." Now amusement danced in his eyes, but then he sobered. "You asked a question before my telephone interrupted. You wanted to know where I felt really at home. I feel at home on the production set. I feel at home in my editing studio. I can be at home anywhere with my laptop and the right software. Home doesn't have to be a specific place."

She wasn't sure about that. She couldn't imagine home being anywhere but on the Rocky D. "Home to me will always be the Rocky D. That's where I learned to have self-worth. That's where I found out what I was really good at, about what I loved to do. Work for me is part of who I am. The bigger part comes from the people around me, how much I care for them and how much they care for me. My life isn't all about work. It's about loving your dad and caring for him, being with my friends and caring about them and even my own father, too. Your world might be bigger on the outside, but I think my world is bigger on the inside."

Cocking his head, Zack assessed her as if he didn't really know her, and maybe he didn't. Just because they'd once been intimate and in love, didn't mean the bonds had lasted, didn't mean they still acted and reacted like those teenagers, didn't mean anything but sexual chemistry remained.

"You could be right. But while you're here, try to enjoy everything so that you can take it back to the inside with you."

As Zack left the room, she realized he'd missed her point. The inside for her wasn't the Rocky D...it was her heart.

Jenny returned to Zack's house as two sleek, black luxury vehicles exited his driveway. After she gathered her packages, she thanked his driver and went inside.

Zack was picking up empty old-fashioned glasses sitting around his living room. "Timed perfectly," he noted, as he tossed her a smile and went to the kitchen.

"I'm going to take these to my room," she said as she passed him.

But he'd already set the glasses in the sink and he caught her arm. "Did you enjoy yourself?"

She would have enjoyed herself more if he'd been with her. "I did. I found great Christmas presents for Celeste, Mikala, Abby and—" she hesitated "—even my dad."

Zack's fingers became more gentle. "Do you think he'll show?"

"I can hope."

Zack took a few of the bags from her arms. "Here, I'll help you."

When the back of his hand grazed her breast, the

contact was searing. His gaze locked to hers, and she didn't think either of them breathed.

Carefully, he grabbed the bags and strode down the hall. She followed him slowly, still tingling from his inadvertent touch. How would she feel if it was more purposeful? How would she feel if she let herself respond as her body wanted to...as her heart wanted to?

He plopped the bags on the yellow settee. "What do you want to do next?"

"How about a walk on the beach?"

He looked surprised she might want to do that and she added, "I want to get a real feel for the ocean."

He tilted his head in agreement. "A walk on the beach it is. Better grab a jacket. It's getting colder."

"Cold is Miners Bluff in January. I think I can handle this."

Again he studied her with something close to penetrating attention. How she wished she knew what kind of thoughts clicked through his mind. But Zack had become an enigma to her and she only caught glimpses of the boy she'd known once in a great while.

The sun was hanging close to the horizon. Gray and purple stole into the sky as they walked without talking from the deck and down the steps to the beach. She thought she might not be able to keep up with Zack, but he didn't seem to be in a hurry.

"Do you do this often?"

"Whenever I can. I often jog on the beach in the morning when I'm here."

"You know what Michael said was true. As much as you like horses, I'm surprised you don't have a place with a couple of them here. You could ride whenever you wanted."

"I'd probably have to move farther north and have a longer commute."

"Wouldn't it be worth it?"

He stopped in the loose sand and faced her. "What are you trying to do, Jenny? Get me to admit I miss the Rocky D?"

"I'm not trying to do that. I just think, well...if I moved my life from the Rocky D, across the country somewhere, I'd still want to be around horses. Our passions are part of us, and whether you admit it or not, when you're gentling Dusty, your passion still shows."

"Out here I have to worry about paparazzi," he grumbled. "Back at the Rocky D, I have to be concerned about you and my dad watching every move I make."

"It's not like that," she protested.

His brows arched. "Try to fit your pretty feet in my shoes."

"You actually think my feet are pretty?" she teased, turning backward, still trying to talk to him as she walked that way. She didn't want to fight. Teasing was more fun.

"I always thought they were. Take your shoes off and feel the sand. Or are you afraid to because your nails are painted fuchsia or lime, or some fashionable color?"

Actually, they were. They were a sparkly purple this week but she certainly didn't want him to know that.

He saw something in her face, though.

"They *are* painted a wild color and you don't want me to know."

"Now, Zack."

He started running after her and then she did take off, running for all her life.

The loose sand and high tufts of grass made running

difficult and she had to make sure she didn't twist an ankle.

He was used to jogging on the sand, used to catching up to anyone he wanted to catch up to.

"You're pretty good," he said when he caught her and twirled her around. "But I beat you, so I get to see your feet."

"I don't think I remember that being part of the deal!"

"We can wait until we go back to my house and I could explore them there."

Out of frustration and some embarrassment, she sank down onto the sand and pulled off her shoe, then her sock. He witnessed the glory of purple nail polish on a foot that seemed demure in every other way. Back in high school, he'd known she wasn't demure, not by the way she responded to his kisses and touches, not the way she'd responded that night they'd made love. Now he looked at her as if he were considering his next move.

His smile crookedly boyish, he said, "I think we should really explore your wild side."

"I don't like that look in your eye."

"You wanted to experience the ocean, right?"

"Zack..."

He scooped her up off the sand and she felt like a rag doll in his arms. She kept protesting, but he didn't hear. Or if he did hear, he was intent on doing what he wanted to do anyway. That was Zack.

And she loved him. She was in love with him all over again.

That realization hit about the same moment he plunged into the cold waves, drenching them both in surf. She screamed, but she found it wasn't in dismay. She screamed, then laughed, because she was enjoying this wild idea of Zack's as much as he was. Laughing, too, he twirled them around and the surf splashed them all over. Then he was running with her back to the shore, back to the safety of just his arms and the California night. She held on tight as he sprinted back to his house. At the bottom of the steps, he set her down but she didn't let go. Her arms were still around his neck as she stood on tiptoe, reaching up to him.

There were no words for that moment. Yes, they were wet and she was starting to shiver, but she could feel Zack's warmth and wanted more of it.

As soon as his lips came down on hers, she wasn't cold. All she could feel was the heat the two of them generated. All she knew was that she didn't want to be separated from this man.

He broke the kiss only to come back for more, again and again and again.

The breeze blew by them and Zack tightened his arms and separated from her for a moment. "We have to get inside and get these clothes off."

She didn't disagree. She took his hand as they ran up the steps, as they crossed the deck, as he tugged her inside the sunroom, away from the surf and the wind. As he kissed her again, her fingers tunneled under his shirt, seeking the warmth of his chest.

He trailed kisses down her neck, but then asked in a murmur, "Are you sure?"

"Oh, yes," she answered, "I'm sure." She'd been fighting to keep her feet under her for too long. She'd been fighting all the feelings that had never been resolved. She'd been fighting the idea of loving Zack again. In his arms, she couldn't imagine why. Responding to his kiss, she didn't even want to think about it.

As they undressed each other, she could hear the ocean. As she rid Zack of his shirt, the last glimmer of daylight faded away. They were surrounded by windows, views of the sea and the scent of each other, damp from their dip, heated from their desire, magnificently unique to them. Zack's body heat almost singed her as she ran her hands over his muscularly developed shoulders, his arms, his flat stomach. He easily stripped her clothes from her, kissing her everywhere skin was revealed until he was kneeling before her, kissing her where she wanted him to touch her most.

Jenny felt weightless as he brought her to orgasm, then caught her as she sank to the floor with him. The rug was soft and silky against her back. Zack was strong and hard and hungry as he stretched out on top of her. They'd been coming to this for weeks, ever since he'd returned. She'd been pushing it away, pushing *him* away, but now she just wanted to be part of him, just wanted to know that what they had was real.

It felt real.

Zack's beard stubble against her face was erotic. The glimmer in his eyes when he tore away from their kiss expressed the passion he was feeling. His lips teased and titillated her body until sensation was her world. He caressed between her legs, checking to see if she was ready for him. She'd been ready for him for years. Although she didn't want to admit it, her dreams were filled with him, her memories of their time together a golden treasure she cherished. She'd done him wrong by not telling him about the baby. She'd done them both wrong.

Zack rose above her, looked deep into her eyes and then entered her. She rose up to meet him, wanting to give him so much of herself she had nothing left. For a few spectacular moments of giving and receiving and joining, they were one. She clung to Zack as her body tensed and then unwound into bliss. After his shuddering release, there was no time or distance between them and they held on, savoring the beauty of what they'd just given each other.

As they lay there, the ocean sounds seemed to grow louder, the night darker, the temperature cooler. Rationality returned with a vehemence when Zack raised his head. "I can't believe I didn't protect you. I can't believe this happened again."

Of course, she knew what he meant. She was concerned, too. But those weren't the first words she wanted to hear out of his mouth. What about, *I still love you?* But as she saw the worry in his eyes, she realized he felt betrayed by her not going with him, and that betrayal could mean he'd never trust her again. The truth was—*could* she follow him anywhere? Could she ever think about leaving the Rocky D?

"I let it happen," she said on a soft sigh. "Protection wasn't only *your* responsibility. Not before and not now."

He rolled to his side but reached for her and brushed her hair behind her ear. "You'd welcome a child, wouldn't you?"

She had to admit she would. Zack's child would mean everything to her. "I didn't let this happen on purpose, if that's what you're thinking. I mean, I wasn't using you to have a baby."

Her blunt words silenced him for a little while.

"Tell me something," she said quietly. "Have you changed your opinion of marriage?"

"You know how I feel about marriage, how I watched Mom and Dad fight. And I've witnessed more divorces than successful unions."

The reality was—she could never change Zack's mind. But she could tell him how she felt about commitment and vows. "I look at Celeste and Clay and I know marriage is about what two people make it. I want to be a wife and mother, doing work I love to do."

"You need commitment."

"I need *more* than commitment. I need vows and a steadfast love."

"That you never had from your dad."

She bristled a little. "I'm an adult now, Zack. I know what I didn't have as a kid. But I know what I want as a woman."

His gaze was steady and probing. "Are you telling me you don't have affairs?"

"I don't have affairs, not unless you count the one I had with you." She sat up and would have risen, but he caught her arm, looking vexed and unsettled.

"I can't be what you want me to be," he said with certainty. "I've made a life here. I brought you to L.A. so you could see it. One of the actors I know is having a premiere tomorrow night. I want you to go with me."

She had to give his life a chance, didn't she? She at least owed him that. "I'll go with you."

"And to the party afterward?"

"And to the party afterward." She would get a good look at Zack's life, up close and personal. But... "I didn't bring anything dressy."

"We can go shopping in the morning. There are plenty of designer boutiques. I'm sure you can find something."

"You'll go with me?"

"Why not? I owe you another pair of shoes. Yours got lost with the tide."

It wasn't only her shoes that had gotten lost with that tide. Memories and thoughts and her convictions had floated away, too.

Tomorrow, maybe she'd like what she saw of Zack's life. Maybe she *could* think about leaving the Rocky D.

Chapter Ten

Jenny ducked into the sumptuously equipped pink-and-black-marble bathroom, heaving a sigh of relief. The red carpet had been exciting yet intimidating. Dressed in an off-shoulder, black beaded designer gown, she'd had more confidence than she'd expected with camera flashes, reporters, fans and paparazzi creating chaos around them. She'd held on to Zack as if he were her lifeline. *He'd* taken it all in with confidence and nonchalance, introducing her to whoever stopped them, making her comfortable when a conversation swirled around them. It was easy to see he was in demand when he was out and about.

Still...she'd gotten the feeling he kept himself removed from all of it. They'd come to this party at the home of one of his "friends" but she'd gotten the feeling they were more acquaintances than really friends.

Jenny studied her reflection in the mirror and spotted a work of art on the wall behind her. It was probably a very *valuable* work of art.

As she plucked her tube of lipstick from her purse, the door to the bathroom opened.

"Oh, sorry," the tall, attractive brunette said. "I didn't know anyone was in here."

Jenny hadn't locked the door since she was just going to freshen up. "No problem," she said with a smile. "As soon as I fix my makeup, I'm out of here."

"I'm Sheila Jameson. You're Jenny, right?"

"Yes," Jenny answered with some surprise, shaking the woman's hand.

"My husband and Zack are business associates. He was at Zack's house yesterday for a meeting on an upcoming project."

"I see." Jenny wasn't sure what else to say.

"There will definitely be talk about you being Zack's flavor of the month."

"Flavor of the month?"

"In the tabloids. When they find out you stayed overnight at his place..." She let her words trail off and shrugged. "Well, you know how it is."

Tabloids. Lord, was she naive. Was her picture going to be in supermarkets? "I'm just an old friend."

"Your history will be laid out if there's any history to find."

Jenny's shock must have shown.

"You're new to this, aren't you? Zack should have prepared you for the aftershock. The truth is I don't think he takes one look at anything anybody writes about him, but everyone else does."

That sounded like Zack. "Have you and your husband known Zack long?"

"A few years, but I can't say we really know him. He's a hard man to get to know." Sheila stepped up to the huge double vanity beside Jenny. "As an old friend, how long have *you* known Zack?"

Jenny hesitated to answer.

"I'll find out tomorrow in the gossip columns," Sheila said with a sideways glance. "It's amazing what a reporter can discover on the internet with a picture and a name."

Jenny applied lipstick to her upper lip and then her lower lip, feeling as if she'd been swallowed up by an alien world. "I've known Zack since high school."

"Oh, there *is* a story here."

When Jenny was about to protest, Sheila shook her head. "No use denying it." She produced a compact. "There's been a lot of speculation about Zack and the women he dates. Rumor has it, he starts an affair with an end in mind. Maybe you're the reason."

In spite of the ring of truth in Sheila's supposition, Jenny felt the need to defend him. "Maybe Zack's just a private person and the rumors are all wrong."

"Maybe, but there's always a hint of truth there."

Dropping her lipstick into her purse, Jenny snapped it shut. "I'd better get back to the party."

"Back to the party...or back to *Zack?*"

Jenny was silent.

Sheila laughed. "You're learning already. It was nice to meet you, Jenny. It's good to know there might be someone in Zack's life who's a little special to him."

Jenny really didn't know what to say to that. After a murmured, "It was good to meet you, too," she exited the powder room, wishing she *had* locked the door behind her.

Reaching the enormous living room with its open gas fireplace and sunken sections, she noticed Zack was in one of those areas speaking to an actor she recognized from a sitcom. Should she approach him or leave him to his conversation? Last night had made everything awkward between them. Not more intimate, not more clarifying, certainly not more definitive.

To her relief, she didn't have to decide whether to approach or not, because Zack saw her, excused himself from his conversation, mounted the two steps and came toward her.

His easy stride, the way he looked in that tuxedo, the concerned look in his eyes practically melted her. He'd wrapped his arms around her heart again. If she tried to wriggle away, if she tried to cut him out of her life once more, she really wasn't sure what would happen.

What if she was pregnant with his baby? Oh, she'd want his child, but a relationship with Zack would become even more complicated than it was. How had she gotten herself into this mess?

By *loving* him, that's how.

When he reached her, he gently took her arm and guided her toward a set of French doors leading to a patio around the pool. Shrugging out of his tuxedo jacket, he dropped it around her shoulders, then opened the door. They stepped outside into a backyard that was as unreal as the rest of the luxurious appearance of the house. A gigantic triple-tiered fountain bubbled and gurgled in blue light while the pool itself shimmered a blue as perfect as the seas. They walked to the wrought-iron railing and stared into the grandeur of marble benches, manicured paths and garden arbors.

"Did you enjoy yourself tonight?" he asked, staring out over all of it.

"It was exciting, being a part of a premiere."

Now she could feel him studying her. "That's not what I asked."

When she turned to face him, she knew she couldn't hide the truth. "It was an experience, Zack, one I'll always remember. I was dazzled. I was busy absorbing it all, trying to keep myself from gawking at all the celebrities, at the designer dresses, at the fabulous shoes." She gave him a smile that was the best she could muster.

"But you wouldn't want to do this often, and you could live your life without it."

She stayed silent until finally she asked, "Did *you* enjoy yourself?"

He didn't answer quickly as she thought he might. "This kind of thing has become such a part of my life, I take it for granted, I guess."

"Can I ask you something without you getting defensive?"

"I don't know if that's such a great way to start. It makes me defensive before you ask. But go ahead."

"How many people do you know here?"

He furrowed his brow. "Oh, Jenny. I work with some, do business with others, attend cocktail parties and benefits with friends of their friends."

"But how many of them do you know? I mean, *really* know? Do you ever sit down and have a conversation about what you did when you were a kid? Do they know you like horses? Do you know what really matters in their lives? Is there anyone here that if you didn't talk to them within the next month, it would matter?"

He went silent and that silence developed into the remote wall that she'd felt since the reunion. "You're becoming defensive, and you're backing away."

"How do you expect me to react to a question like that?" Frustration was evident in his voice.

"I was hoping you could answer it. I was hoping that there was someone here who matters as much as Dawson and Clay, Mikala and Celeste, me and your dad."

"Maybe I've decided that those kinds of ties cost too much."

She gazed into the end-of-November night, not knowing what to say.

Taking hold of her shoulder, he nudged her around to face him again. "Can't you let go of the Rocky D and Miners Bluff for just one night?"

Biting her lower lip, she sifted through her feelings before she confessed, "I let go of it last night, Zack, only to find out I had nothing else to hang on to when I did. I'm ready to go home."

He looked frustrated with her, but the fire was back in his eyes as if he wanted to kiss her. Then, all at once, his face became neutral, his tone even. "I'll find our host and we can say our goodbyes."

She was afraid she was saying more than goodbye to L.A. She was afraid she was starting to say goodbye to Zack all over again.

Instead of bales of hay and the rustic look of a barn, the firehouse's social hall was buzzing on Friday afternoon with volunteers who were filling food baskets and taking deliveries to needy families in the area. Back in Miners Bluff again, Jenny and Zack worked side by side, speaking to the other volunteers but not each other. There was a crackle in the air when their gazes met, current rushing between them if they inadvertently touched. But Jenny was keeping her thoughts and words to herself and so was Zack.

Anna stopped beside Jenny and gave the two of them a wise, knowing look. "Silas says he's doing well with his rehab."

Zack responded, "He says his nurse is a slave driver but he's looking better every day."

"That's wonderful. I hope he can start looking forward again and see what he can accomplish. He thinks his best years are behind him, but that isn't so." She paused, then said, "Mikala tells me you were in California for a few days." She looked at Zack. "I bet you miss it."

"I miss the ocean and the long walks on the beach. But as far as work, I'm amazed at what I can accomplish long distance. With smart phones and video conferencing, work really is portable."

"Mikala does that video conferencing on her computer. I don't understand the first thing about it." Anna tapped her pocket. "But I wouldn't be without my cell phone. It's my connection to Mikala and all my friends. I even text."

Jenny laughed. "Maybe you can teach Silas how to do it. I've tried to, but he just gives me one of those looks and says talking's good enough for him."

"I'll keep that in mind." Anna's eyes twinkled. "I'll be seeing him Sunday. I'm picking him up and we're going to dinner."

At Jenny and Zack's astonished silence, she said, "I see he didn't tell you."

"It's wonderful you're going out!" Jenny said, recovering from her surprise.

Anna blushed a little. "Just to the Feather Peak Diner."

"An outing will be good for Dad. I should have thought of it myself," Zack said, seeming sincere.

"We made plans while you were gone. But I thought he'd tell you."

Jenny suspected why Silas hadn't. Maybe he thought Zack wouldn't approve.

Anna noticed the baskets Zack and Jenny had almost completed filling. "Would you mind delivering some of these? We've so many this year."

Jenny gazed up at Zack and he gave a small shrug and a nod. "Sure, I have the truck," he agreed. "We'll load it up and we'll be on our way."

Fifteen minutes later, they were on the road, Zack expertly driving.

"What do you think of your dad and Anna going out?"

Zack gave an offhanded shrug. "He enjoyed Anna's company on Thanksgiving. Maybe while we were gone he decided he can have a real life again."

"How will you feel if they become serious?" she pressed.

"Dad's never consulted me about his decisions. I don't think he'll start now."

Zack was so good at evading what he felt as well as talking about it. Jenny let the subject alone for now. "I tagged one of the baskets for the Larsons."

Zack gave her a quick sideways look. "From what Michael says, I don't think his dad would appreciate it."

"I don't know if he'll appreciate it or not, but they need it. Maybe they won't be home and we can just leave the basket at the door."

"If Mr. Larson is home, we'll deal with him." Zack's quick look was confident.

"Just because you can convince Dusty to come inside the barn now, doesn't mean you can get Stan Larson to accept a handout without protest."

"There's a secret. Dusty doesn't have to stay inside the barn. That door to the corral is always open. He can come and go as he pleases. You just have to give a person an out so they don't feel trapped."

"And what's the out we're going to give Stan Larson?"

"Let me work on it," Zack said with a wry smile.

Jenny just shook her head.

After a few quiet minutes, Jenny knew she had to fill Zack in on plans she'd made for Sunday. "Clay, Celeste and Abby are coming over Sunday afternoon. Will you be around?"

"*Should* I be around?"

She shifted uncomfortably because she realized he probably knew she had something in mind besides a simple visit. "I told Abby we'd make cookies and I thought maybe you and Clay could set up the tree. Hank and Ben found one that's perfect. It's in the storage shed for now."

Zack's silence was telling. He'd already explained holidays meant little to him. But she was trying to change that and he knew it.

Finally, he answered, "It will be good to spend some time with Clay and Celeste."

She noticed he didn't mention Abby. Because it was too painful to think about the child they'd lost and dwell on what could have been?

Two hours later, they'd delivered all the baskets except for the one Jenny had put together for Michael and Tanya's family. Zack had been on his phone on and off in between deliveries and had even let her drive some of the way. She wasn't sure what the calls were about. She couldn't quite tell from his side of the conversations.

As they approached the address Jenny had secured from her lesson roster, she began to feel a little nervous. What if Michael's dad *was* home?

Once again in the driver's seat, she asked Zack, "Are we making a mistake?"

"This is food we're talking about, Jenny. I suspect this family is making do and not by very much. We can at least try. If the help is rejected, we'll find another way to help."

After they disembarked from the truck, Zack pulled the lone basket from the back. Then he slammed the truck's bed door shut. When they reached the front door, Jenny punched the bell and waited, hoping Helen would answer.

But luck wasn't with her today. Stan Larson opened the door, studied them for a few minutes, then scowled. "Aren't you from the Rocky D?"

"Yes, we are," Jenny answered, her shoulders squared, her gaze meeting the proud man's. "But really, today we're just from Miners Bluff. We're passing out food baskets and we'd like to give you one."

"My family is fine," he said stiffly. "Go give your basket to someone else."

"Maybe we should introduce ourselves," Zack interjected. "This is Jenny Farber and I'm Zack Decker."

"I know who you are. Don't you think I hear from Helen how great Miss Farber is with the kids? Don't you think I know she's giving them lessons for free? And you...I've seen your face on TV and in magazines. I don't want your food. I don't need it."

Zack set the basket down on the porch floor then straightened slowly. "You're a father, Mr. Larson. Isn't it your job to provide the best you can?"

Jenny took hold of Zack's elbow. "Zack."

But Michael and Tanya's dad shook his head. "Let him say his piece, then he can leave with his basket. I'm not a charity case."

"Isn't it true you're out of work?" Zack pressed.

"I am, but I'll have a job soon. I'm waiting to hear from a couple of friends."

"How far are you behind on your rent, your utilities?"

"That's none of your business."

"Maybe not, but I don't think you want to lose everything, including the respect of your family, do you?"

"What would *you* know about it?"

The way he said the word "you," Jenny was sure Michael's dad thought Zack lived in another universe.

"You're right, I don't know how you feel," Zack admitted. "I had plenty lean years when I didn't have work. Thank God, I didn't have a family to take care of then. But you do. So I don't think you can afford to let pride rule your life."

"You think a ham and some canned goods are going to make a difference?"

"It might in the way you spend your holiday, and what you have to be thankful for. But maybe I'm here to offer you more than a food basket."

Jenny dashed a look at Zack in total surprise. What was he talking about?

From Stan Larson's expression, he wondered the same thing.

"Are you willing to change your life?" Zack asked.

"What does that mean?" Stan was definitely wary.

"Are you willing to move to Phoenix?"

Michael's dad took a step back. "I...I don't know. Why?"

"I have a contact in Phoenix who owns a general contracting company. He's managed to ride out the economic downturn when other companies have gone under. He has several crews and he could use a qualified electrician. Are you interested?"

Stan looked speechless, and then he looked mystified. "Why would you do this? You don't know me."

"I know Tanya and I know Michael, and they seem to think you're a good dad who just needs a break. I know they'll miss everyone here if you move, but in the long run, life could be better for them. Right?"

Zack produced a card from his pocket and handed it to the man. "Dawson Barrett is the CEO of the company. His dad, Greg Barrett, is his crew manager and right-hand man. Both of their numbers are on there. Give either one of them a call today and they'll give you the details. They're looking to hire soon, so you have to make up your mind."

Stan studied the card, turning it over in his hand. "I have to talk to Helen."

"Of course you do," Zack acknowledged. "Dawson said you could call their cell numbers."

"Helen took the kids downtown to McDougall's Department Store to see Santa. I told her it wasn't any point. She was setting them up for disappointment."

"Maybe now they won't have to be disappointed," Jenny said softly. "There's a gift certificate to McDougall's in the basket. Please don't look on this as charity. Just try to look at it as the people of Miners Bluff standing together to help each other."

Stan stared down at his sneakers. "I suppose the rich folk of Miners Bluff donated all this."

"No," Jenny told him quickly. "That's not true. Everybody in town gave what they could. Maybe sometime soon, you'll be able to help someone who needs a hand up."

Stan's gaze went to the basket, rose to Zack's and then Jenny's. "I don't know how to thank you."

"Dawson's a high school buddy of mine," Zack told him. "Just do a good job for him."

Stan stooped to pick up the basket and then smiled at them for the first time. "I can't wait 'til Helen gets home."

As they turned away, Jenny tossed over her shoulder, "Tell her I'll see her tomorrow for the kids' lessons." He waved as they climbed into the truck. He was still waving as they drove away.

On the road again, out of the corner of his eye, Zack could see Jenny swing around as far as she could with her seat belt attached. "You didn't tell me you were going to do that," she accused.

"I didn't know if it would come together. Dawson might not have needed anyone. He had to check with his dad and wait to hear back. I didn't want you to be disappointed."

Jenny was quiet as Zack drove back to the Rocky D, and he didn't know what to think. Did she believe he had been too high-handed? Sometimes it was hard to tell with her these days. She was doing a better job of keeping her guard up.

He thought about their walk on the beach and what had happened afterward in Malibu. No guard up then… for either of them. Was that why he backed away from everything she'd tried to tell him? Was that why the idea of commitment urged him to work through the night and most of the day, too? She wanted so much and he felt as if he could give so little.

He kept thinking everything would have been different if she'd gone with him to L.A. when he'd asked her. Yet, would everything *really* have been different? Would she have stayed? Or would she have bailed? Would she have gotten tired of waiting for him to ask her to marry him when that had never been in his plans? Would he have started thinking differently about a life with her? Especially if she was pregnant.

And what if she was pregnant now? That thought practically made him panic and he wasn't the panicking type.

He'd always known his own mind. He'd always had goals and known exactly what they were. Now, his life was fuzzy. He was restless and not much made sense.

He drove under the wooden sign for the Rocky D that marked the front boundary of the property as he had done thousands of times before. At least, since his dad's heart attack, he didn't feel so estranged from his life here as a kid. He definitely didn't feel as estranged from Jenny.

The lane was rutted with tire tracks. He tried his best not to give them a rough ride, but he knew they were in for one anyway. They couldn't put a stop to this attraction any more than they could stop breathing. Staying away from each other, in some ways, just made the chemistry even more obvious.

Chemistry. He'd never felt this kind of chemistry with any woman other than Jenny and that was way too telling on its own.

Zack had no sooner pressed the remote to park the truck in one of the garages, when Jenny unfastened her seat belt. He thought she was in a hurry to jump out and get busy doing whatever else she wanted to do for the day. Jenny was like that. She never sat idle. Yet, instead, she waited for him to switch off the ignition. To his surprise, she leaned over, wrapped her arms around his neck and kissed him full on the lips.

Reacting instinctively, he unhitched his seat belt with one hand and wrapped his other arm around her. Kissing across the console wasn't the most comfortable position in the world, but comfort was the last thing on his mind as fire raced through him, as sensations jammed his brain and all he could think about was leading Jenny to his bed.

She let up first and he told himself this wasn't the place to go crazy, tear her clothes off, or to pretend they were those teenagers again.

When his thoughts got unstuck, he took a deep breath, righted himself in his seat and asked, "What was that for?"

"That was for the wonderful thing you did for Michael and Tanya. Do you know what this means for them and their future?"

He felt heat creeping up his neck at her praise and strived to be offhanded. "I checked around Miners Bluff and even in Flagstaff before I made the call to Dawson. I couldn't find him anything else."

"If they get back on their feet, the economy picks up and they want to move back here in a few years, they can. But they'll build a life wherever they go and that's what's important," she concluded.

"Is that what's important?" he asked and watched to see if Jenny caught the underlying meaning of his message.

Before she could answer him, his cell phone buzzed. Jenny motioned for him to take it and he checked the caller ID.

"It's work," he said, wanting to hear her answer.

But she was already climbing out of the truck. He knew why. She didn't want to answer his question because it came too close to the root of the problems between them.

Ten minutes later, he went into the house, knowing his call would make everything between them more complicated. Jenny was in the kitchen having a glass of orange juice at the counter. She'd taken off her coat. Her Western-motif red and green sweater hugged her slim body at the waistband of her jeans. Her high boots showed off her slim legs. She'd worn her hair in a ponytail today and with the cold air still pinking her cheeks, she looked like the all-American western girl. The kiss was still with him and he was glad his sheepskin jacket fell midthigh. He didn't unsnap it.

She must have been able to tell something from his expression because she asked, "Problem?"

"No. In fact, it was good news about the documentary project I want to do."

"Concerning veterans?"

"Yes, the funding's there, but...I'm going to be traveling for the next few months."

"Traveling?"

"I can put the production company together long distance from here. I know who I want on my team. But this is all about the men's stories so I'm going to have a lot of interviews to do, many of them in D.C., some across the country."

"Do you want to do the interviews yourself?"

"I'm not sure about that yet, but I do know I want to run the project, as well as edit it, not stay in the background. It will air in about a year on a cable network."

The disappointment in Jenny's eyes was obvious and he approached her and stood beside her. "I can't delay the timing of this. It's too important."

"Silas is on the mend," she offered with sudden neutrality that made him want to shake her.

"I was hoping I could convince you to spend some time in California, maybe in the spring," he offered.

"That's when the Rocky D's the busiest."

"The Rocky D is busy all year." He had to let her know she couldn't use that as an excuse.

Her eyes were brimming with the turmoil she was feeling. "And if I spend time with you in California in the spring, what would that mean?" The question came spurting out of her as if it had just been waiting to erupt.

"I don't know, Jen. I don't have the answers."

She backed away from him. "Well, I need some answers, Zack. Soon I'll know if I'm pregnant or not, but that doesn't make our situation any clearer."

"Life isn't about clarity. It's about taking what you have and working with it," he responded gruffly.

"You don't want marriage and a family and traditions to pass down. I do."

But Jenny didn't want to leave the Rocky D. They were back to square one.

Chapter Eleven

Zack wasn't sure when the idea of Christmas approaching had started to mean something to him—when he'd seen his mother's golden bells in the barn, heard them jingling in the wind, or when Jenny had hung a wreath on the front door.

As he held a huge, nine-foot fir steady in the Rocky D's living room on Sunday afternoon and Clay Sullivan tightened the screws holding the trunk in place, he smelled the aroma of cinnamon and cookies baking emanating from the kitchen.

Christmas. What would it mean this year?

"Five bucks for your thoughts," Clay said, as he stood and studied Zack as well as the tree.

"Not worth that," he said with a grimace.

"It must be difficult for you being back here after all this time."

The tree supported now, Zack stepped away from it. "Actually, each day's gotten easier. I guess part of me missed winter and the horses and memories I'd tried to bury."

"How are you and Silas?"

"Peaceful for the moment, but that might not last, especially when I tell him I'm leaving January second."

Clay didn't comment on that, but rather helped Zack gather trimmed tree boughs. Finally he said, "Parents understand more than you think. They want to protect us and keep us close. They just don't always know how to do that without interfering."

"You said you and your dad have gotten closer."

"Celeste had everything to do with that."

"Jenny believes my father is a changed man, and even though her own dad has disappointed her over and over, she keeps the door open for him."

"Maybe women are just more forgiving."

"Maybe."

"What's bothering you, Zack? Something's on your mind today. It's obvious."

Zack raked his hand through his hair and decided his long friendship with Clay was worth a lot. "After I left the Rocky D, Jenny found out she was pregnant. But then she had a miscarriage. I found out about it after Dad's heart attack."

Clay's eyes widened with surprise. "That had to feel like a sucker punch."

"It did. She didn't trust me enough to tell me. She didn't trust me enough to go with me, either, so maybe I shouldn't be so surprised."

"She was only eighteen."

Why couldn't he let go of it? Why couldn't he let go of Jenny?

Because nothing had changed. He'd be leaving, and she'd be staying despite chemistry and memories and connections.

Suddenly, Abby came running into the long living room like a miniature tornado. Stopping beside Clay, she looked up at the tree and clapped her hands. "It's up."

"Sure is," Zack said with a smile for Clay's almost-four-year-old daughter. "As soon as we wrap it with some lights, it's all yours."

The hairs on Zack's neck prickled as Jenny walked in. He was more aware of Jenny now than he'd ever been. Celeste followed her with steaming mugs of hot chocolate on a tray. Clay's wife was a quietly pretty woman with light brown hair and green eyes. At first a surrogate mother to Abby, now she was her real mother. Clay didn't talk about his ex-wife, Zoie—Celeste's twin sister—very much, but Zack knew Zoie was now in and out of Abby's life like a favorite aunt and they were all happy.

As soon as Celeste set the tray of hot chocolate mugs on a side table, Clay wrapped his arm around her. They did appear to be substantially happy.

Carrying an ivory china Christmas plate with painted poinsettias—Zack recognized it as one of his mom's favorites—Jenny offered him a cookie. While he and Clay wrestled with the tree, Celeste, Jenny and Abby had been baking and decorating cookies. He now could choose from pink angels with yellow wings to blue stars with lots of sprinkles to a reindeer with green icing and an almost-red nose.

"You've been busy."

Jenny's gaze met his and for an instant, just an instant, he saw the intimate knowledge there of a man and woman who'd slept together. In a blink, it was gone and Jenny was making conversation as if that knowledge was something she wanted to forget.

"Did you tell Clay about your new project?" she asked Zack with enthusiasm that seemed a little bit too robust.

"He did," Clay answered seriously. "I think our veterans need a documentary like that."

"Look what I found," Abby announced from across the room.

Cardboard boxes full of Christmas decorations were lined up against the sofa. Zack had carried them down this morning. One of the cartons was home for the Christmas lights, but the one Abby had opened held ornaments. She removed a porcelain ornament with a horse painted on it. When he spotted it, he wanted to snatch it from Abby and bury it in the box again. But he couldn't, of course.

Celeste was running to her daughter saying, "Oh, be careful, honey."

Zack rounded the other side of the box and crouched down beside Abby, sliding his large hand under the ornament. "That's a very old one."

"How old?" Abby asked.

"About sixteen years old. It was my Christmas present to my mom one year."

"Where *is* your mommy?" Abby asked with all the innocence most children possessed.

Suddenly, Jenny was beside Abby, too, hunkering

down beside Zack. When he seemed at a loss, she answered, "Zack's mom is in heaven."

"Where the angels are?" Abby asked.

"That's right," Celeste said gently. She pointed to the ornament to veer the conversation away from a sensitive topic. "And that was Zack's mom's favorite horse. One of his friends painted it for him so he could give it to her."

"Brenna," Jenny said remembering.

Zack remembered Brenna McDougall and the ornament and that Christmas that had seemed so special because he and Jenny had spent a lot of time together. His chest tightened and he concentrated on conversation that wasn't so touchy.

"Did anyone talk to Brenna at the reunion?" he asked. "I caught sight of her dancing with Riley and was surprised." There had been problems between the McDougalls and O'Rourkes and it had been an oddity to see Brenna and Riley together when they'd kept their distance in high school.

"I just talked to her for a little while," Jenny said. "She has put all of her artistic talent to good use. She designs bridal gowns now, and is quite famous in her own right."

Abby pointed to the ornament. "Can I hang this on the tree?"

Zack stepped in right away so no one else had to. "Sure you can. As soon as we get those lights attached. Just give us fifteen minutes and we'll be ready for you."

When Abby looked disappointed she couldn't do it right away, Jenny reminded her, "We have to go roll those peanut butter balls in the chocolate chips."

"Can I eat one?" Abby asked.

"Sounds like something we'll all want to eat," Clay said with a laugh.

"Jenny made the hot chocolate with real chocolate," Celeste told her husband, "so I think you'll like it. Don't let it get cold."

"I won't. Like Zack said, just give us fifteen minutes then we'll be ready to decorate the tree."

"Can we play carols?" Abby's gaze targeted Zack because he seemed to be the one in charge.

Right now, he didn't want to be the one in charge. This afternoon with Clay and Celeste and Abby was becoming more than he'd bargained for. Yet, he wouldn't let down this little girl for anything.

"Sure, we can. I'll bet Jenny has a stack of them somewhere."

"From Elvis to Jewel," Jenny assured Abby and crooked her finger at her. "Come on, I'll show you where they are."

Celeste followed Jenny and Abby out of the room and Zack found he was still holding the ornament.

"I'm sorry Abby got into the box," Clay apologized.

Zack settled the ornament on the coffee table. "That's what kids do—they explore. That will be just another ornament on the tree."

Clay gave him a level look, but Zack ignored it just as he ignored the heart-lancing memories that he'd kept under lock and key for all these years.

A half hour later, Jenny and Celeste brought in not only more cookies to sample, but what Celeste called healthy food, too. There were veggies and dip, whole wheat crackers and cheese, barbecued meat on tiny sandwich rolls.

"We just did this backward," Jenny said with a smile,

and Zack could have kissed her, right then and there. Yet, something stopped him. Those walls around his heart? Other people in the room? Or disconcerting emotions he'd been battling all day?

Abby hung ornaments with enthusiasm, her soft brown curls bobbing around her face, the tiny red bow in her hair swinging as she tilted her head first one way then the other until she picked a perfect branch for each ornament. Jenny had found a CD player and set it on a table. Strains of "Rocking Around the Christmas Tree" were a backdrop to their conversation.

"I'm really having a great time putting together a family history with Clay's mom," Celeste told Zack. "The history of the Sullivans is fascinating. Did you ever think of interviewing your dad and capturing his memories on videotape?"

"I never did," Zack admitted.

"Where *is* Silas?" Clay asked.

"He and Anna Conti went to dinner."

When Clay's eyebrows arched, Zack shrugged. "They're old friends."

While Zack's fingers fumbled with some of the oldest ornaments that reminded him of days gone by, Clay revealed the process he was going through to interview potential partners for his wilderness guiding service.

"It has to be just the right person, not too bookish and not too extreme, someone who really gets along with people."

"Would you consider a woman?" Jenny asked.

Clay shook his head. "I'd be more comfortable with a male partner." He raised a hand before the women could protest. "That's not just chauvinism. I don't want misunderstandings."

"Do you think I'd be jealous?" Celeste teased.

"Well, would you?" Clay joked back.

"That depends on what she looked like and how she acted around you."

"See what I mean?" he muttered. "Besides that, this town's too small to take any chances with gossip."

Just then, Abby brought the porcelain horse ornament over to Zack. "Up, Uncle Zack! I wanna hang it on top."

Uncle Zack. He liked the sound of that. "Okay, honey. Let's see how high we can go." He held her in his arms while Jenny looked on. He could see Jenny's eyes mist up and he could only imagine what she was thinking. Their son or daughter would have made Christmas special, too.

Suddenly, a deep voice said from the doorway, "We hang that on the tree every year. Find a really good spot for it."

Still holding Abby steady, Zack turned to see his father. Apparently, he remembered the ornament, too.

Everyone greeted Silas and then Abby asked, "Here?" as she tried the third branch in a row.

"Looks good," Silas agreed.

She let the ornament swing from the branch.

Zack lowered her to the floor, kissed her forehead and said, "Good job. Now why don't we see how everything looks all lit up?"

As "Have Yourself a Merry Little Christmas" played on the CD player, Zack plugged in the lights. White twinkles danced all around the evergreen and the expression on Abby's face was priceless. Her mouth rounded in a little O, and she just stared at the tree.

Finally, she looked at Clay. "Can we have one like this?"

"Maybe not quite as big as this, but I'll see what I can do."

Zack felt that tightness in his chest again. As his gaze met his dad's, he saw a look of longing on his father's face. What was that about? Regrets? He certainly had a trunkful of his own. Maybe the way he'd handled his father all these years was in that stack.

Crossing to him, Jenny asked in a low voice, "What do you think of Christmas now?"

Her soft brown eyes seemed to try to see into his very soul. He'd never felt closer to her or more distant from her and that was crazy.

"I think Christmas is what we make it. We can't expect too much of it or we'll be disappointed."

She looked disappointed in what he'd said and he suddenly wished he could take it back. Because the truth was—this afternoon maybe he'd understood the true meaning of Christmas. Yet, if he'd told her that, he'd feel too damn vulnerable. And that was the last thing he wanted to feel around Jenny right now.

Jenny made her rounds of the horses almost every night before she turned in. It was a ritual that was necessary not only for her peace of mind, but for Silas's, too. They both had their favorites and that last check of the night told them all was well. Hank, Tate and Ben were always on the alert for problems, though they usually had an apple or carrot stick in their pocket for a bit of conversation with their favorite horse, too. Jenny's walk through the barns was a labor of love that sometimes cut into her sleeping time.

Tonight, however, she had a lot on her mind. The day had been brimming with emotion, from making cookies with Abby, watching her hang Olivia's ornament on the Christmas tree, to seeing the lights go on and everyone's response to them. Silas had been super quiet after his return home. Zack had seemed not so much remote as just very far away. Still, whenever their eyes met or their fingers brushed, the smoking hot electricity between them didn't quit. For her, the idea of his leaving again created an even deeper hole in her heart than the one he'd left so many years ago. She loved him now with a woman's love and still wasn't sure what that meant. Should she grab every moment she could with him? Should she go with him to California and leave the Rocky D? How could Silas ever manage without her?

Letting herself into Songbird's stall, lowering herself to the fresh straw, she asked the horse, who was her closest friend in the stable, "What should I do, Songbird?"

In a corner of the stall, Songbird munched from her feedbox. Jenny could *really* use a little input. When her horse's soft brown eyes seemed to study her with old-soul wisdom, Jenny asked, "You think I should grab love when I can, don't you?"

Songbird gave a soft whinny.

"And just where would that leave you if I took off for the luxurious life?"

She remembered the premiere and the paparazzi, the lights and the questions, the designer gowns and the glittering jewels.

The barn's night creaks and rustlings were interrupted by the outside door opening and then closing.

She hoped it was Zack. She stayed put, knowing if he wanted to find her, he would.

But it wasn't Zack who peeked over the stall. It was Silas. "I thought I'd find you here."

She pushed herself up from the straw. "I came out here to think."

"Accomplishing anything?"

"Not much."

"I bet all your thoughts surround my son."

"Most of them," she admitted. "Can I ask you something?"

"You know you can."

"You knew us both back then. If I had gone with Zack, do you think we would have made it? Do you think we'd still be together?"

Silas unlatched the stall door so Jenny could step out, then he closed it again. "Olivia and I talked about the two of you."

At Jenny's raised brows, he said, "We didn't fight *all* the time, in spite of the way Zack remembers it."

"What if I had left with him? What if I had found out I was pregnant after I was gone when we were together out there? Would he still have been so hell-bent against marriage? Would he have tried to be a father? Could I have been a good mother?"

"Whoa," Silas said, holding up both hands. "Let's take a bit broader look. Zack was determined to succeed so he could wipe my face in it...so he could see his mother's approval. If you had gone with him, I believe he would have wanted you to be part of that, whether a baby was in the mix or not. So then the question becomes—what would have happened through the hard years? Personally, I think you're just as determined as he is. I think you would have stood by him and become the kind of woman who knows how to hold a family together. That's what I believe, Jenny. Both of you have grit and motivation. I've seen it. And let's face it, you had a lot of feelings that needed a place to grow."

"I'm the one who spoiled everything. If I had taken the risk and said yes, I might have the child and family I'd always wanted."

"How would you have felt if Zack hadn't wanted to marry you, even with a baby? Out there, propriety isn't what it is here."

"I don't know how I would have dealt with that. I really don't know. I guess it would have depended if we were the substance of his life, or on the periphery of it...if he was there to promote himself and his career and the life he wanted to make, or if he was really there to take us along with him."

"See? You don't have the answers and you never will. The only way you'll have answers is to do something and take the consequences, whatever they are, and work with them."

As Silas studied her, she felt self-conscious. "What?" she asked.

"I know what you're worrying about."

"I have so many worries you couldn't even begin to count them."

"You know what I mean," he chided. "You're worried about *me*. You can't worry about me. I'm doing better each day. You have to go after what you want, Jenny, or it will slip right through your fingers. Regrets mount up and you want as few as possible when you get to my age."

"You're still young," she said, believing it.

"I'm still young enough to have some years left to enjoy. But I'm also old enough to see the end of my life. That puts perspective on everything. Have you heard whether your dad will be here for Christmas?"

Jenny's heart squeezed a little at the mention of her dad. "I have no idea. I know he has to make money to live on and that's what he's doing with his rodeo technique courses. But just one Christmas I'd love it if he put me first. Selfish, isn't it?"

"You deserve to be selfish. I can't believe you aren't bitter like Zack."

She jumped in quickly. "I don't think he's bitter anymore."

"But he's still leaving."

"I know."

"He's out with Dusty if you want to go to him."

She'd had no idea Zack was with Dusty, but maybe he didn't want to return to the silence of *his* room, either.

After she gave Silas a quick hug, she headed out of the barn.

Jenny found Zack sitting on top of the fence, even though a breeze whipped across the corral. Olivia's jingle bells sounded in the distance. Dusty stood about ten feet from Zack, nosing a clump of grass sticking out from a patch of snow. Had Zack been talking to Dusty the same way she'd been talking to Songbird? He said he was happy with his life. He said Christmas was what he made it.

As quietly as she could, she stepped outside of the barn and walked along the inside perimeter of the fence. Dusty knew her now and shouldn't be spooked by her presence. He lifted his head and eyed her, then returned to munching.

"It's a little cold to be communing with nature," she advised, the night chill already nipping her nose.

Zack's sheepskin collar was turned up and his gloved hands were jammed into his pockets. His Stetson rode low over his brow. The outside barn light barely reached them and his face was in shadows. "Dusty doesn't seem to mind the cold and I thought—" he gave a half shrug "—the winter air would clear my head."

"What are you trying to clear it of?" Her breath made a white puff as she spoke.

When his answer was a swish of the pines and a dark silence, she asked, "Of memories?"

He glanced at her and she felt a warm stirring in her belly. The temperature might be dipping into the thirties but the heat between them never ceased.

"It's odd," he said, looking away again, back at Dusty. "All these years, I thought I remembered everything exactly the way it was. But then today, finding Mom's ornament—" He shook his head as if he still couldn't clear it, as if he still couldn't see straight. "I remember the day Dad gave Mom that horse. His name was Quicksilver, a beautiful Appaloosa. I was fourteen and I remember videotaping her riding him. I think all those tapes are packed in the crawl space on the second floor."

"Maybe you need to watch them, to get the real picture of what your life was."

"I was a kid whose parents fought over my dad's affairs and gambling."

"But not all the time."

"Jeez, Jen, you see the world through rose-colored glasses."

She felt hurt by his comment and tried not to be. She tried to keep her face a mask because Zack was too good at reading her.

He climbed down off the fence a little too quickly and Dusty took a turn around the corral. Pulling off his gloves, Zack stuffed them into his pocket, then took her face between his palms. They felt warm against her cold cheeks. They felt warm because this was Zack and she wanted him to touch her.

"I don't know how you squeeze the best out of everything," he wondered. "You should be bitter about your mom dying, your dad leaving you for weeks at a time, a neighbor who looked after you not caring if there was decent food on the table. You were close to my mother and you lost her, too, yet somehow you remember the good about that and you've left the sadness behind."

Zack thought her leaving the past came naturally without a price. But that wasn't true. "Maybe I remember the good because I accepted feelings as they came. I was lonely and knew it. I felt abandoned and cried through it. I lost my mom and your mom but I didn't deny the grief. Ever since I've known you, Zack, you close down when you're in a situation that makes you feel lonely or uncomfortable or sad. You pack it all away and pretend it doesn't matter. It *does* matter. It will come back to haunt you if you don't live in the moment with it."

"So that's your secret? To live in the moment?"

"I try."

Dusty trotted by them and clomped into the stall that would give him protection against the weather.

As if the moment had gotten too intense, Zack dropped his hands from her face. They both turned to watch the horse.

"I think he's been spending more time in there," Jenny said. "That means he's beginning to feel safe here."

"He's fine as long as no one closes that stall door. If it's closed, he feels trapped."

Was that why Zack couldn't seem to settle in one place? Because if he did, he would feel trapped?

All at once, she was overwhelmed by the love she felt for him. If he was leaving in January, so be it. They had now and didn't now matter?

Closing the distance between their bodies, she looked up at him, reached out and stroked his beard stubble, the cleft in his jaw. "Maybe *we* should go inside, too."

His gaze filled with the desire she'd seen there before. She could feel the pulse in his jawline thumping under her fingers.

"Inside the house or inside the barn?" he prompted.

"The house is awfully far away."

Swinging her up into his arms, he carried her over the uneven ground and strode through the barn's back door to one of the empty stalls strewn with clean hay. The wind whistled in eaves and she heard the swish of Dusty's hooves as he shuffled around his stall.

Zack moved away and came back with a blanket to lay on the straw and another to cover them. Without thinking, Jenny removed her down parka then kept her gaze on Zack as he removed his sheepskin jacket. Watching each other undress was a turn-on, much different from their wild desire on the beach in Malibu, their fast and furious lovemaking that had been more instinct than forethought.

When Zack lay down beside her, she didn't hurry to remove his sweater. Rather, she gazed into his eyes as she ran her hands over him.

He swallowed hard, then in a husky voice said, "You don't get to have all the fun."

His large hands mirrored what she was doing to him until his palms settled on her breasts, until he ran them over her nipples, until she wanted their clothes off as fast as they'd discarded them in his sunroom. But he'd taken his cue from her and Zack wasn't hurrying this time. No, apparently this time, his aim was optimal pleasure.

When he leaned in to kiss her, she was surrounded by the outdoor scent of pine and cold air, the earthy scent of Zack himself. His lips took a slow tour of hers and his tongue eased into her mouth. She clenched a fist-ful of his heavy sweater, the wool coarse against her palm. At first she thought about their tryst in the hay-loft when they were only eighteen, but past memories soon gave way to new ones. Zack was a complicated man now. His passion aged and deepened by experi-ence. Hers rippled under the surface until he kissed her or touched her and brought it hungrily to life.

When he broke away for a moment, she rubbed her nose into his neck and breathed in his scent. Everything about him was wondrously familiar yet different, too. Although he seemed to be in no hurry, she wanted him to need like she did, wanted him to feel restless and hot until their joining was necessary for him to live. She re-leased her grip on his sweater and slid her hand below his waist. He was hard and huge and she rubbed her fingers against his fly until he groaned. He captured her mouth once again and ravished it with his desire. After that, he quickly unsnapped her jeans and she unbelted his. He shucked off his boots while she tugged off hers. They didn't speak because they had nothing to say. They'd gone over it all. They didn't want to debate or argue. They wanted to make love.

Have sex? a little voice asked her. But she ignored it. At this moment, both were one and the same. Maybe later... Later slid into the same place as doubts and worries and consequences. This time Zack protected her. This time she saw something in his eyes that gave her hope.

After he slid on the condom, he stretched out on his back and pulled her on top of him. "You ride," he said. "The straw can poke through the blanket. I don't want it to scratch you."

That had happened before. She'd had red streaks all over her back. He was protecting her and she loved that about him. Had he forgiven her for choosing a life here at the Rocky D? Had he forgiven her for not telling him about the baby?

She hoped so. Oh, how she hoped so.

They were both naked from the waist down. He slid his hands under her sweater and gripped her hips. She lowered herself onto him slowly, taking him in, closing her eyes, holding her breath. She began moving up and down and his hands caressed her as she did. They rocked together, their pace increasing as the heat built. Before, *ecstasy* had merely been a word in the dictionary. Now, it was a reality, wrapping itself around her, bringing a flush to her cheeks and a trembling to her limbs. Her climax was so sudden, blinding and earth-shaking that she felt her voice shatter as she called his name. He climaxed moments later and shuddered as she leaned forward to hold him. Clinging to each other, Jenny realized what living in the moment meant.

Living in the moment was wonderful until the moment passed. After the moment passed, she had to make a crucial decision about the rest of her life.

Chapter Twelve

Jenny had spent the night in Zack's room. It had been a wonderful night of being held...of being loved. At least that's the way she'd seen it. They hadn't talked. They'd just kissed and sighed and touched and groaned with the pleasure they could give each other. But the night had been about more than pleasure. She'd slipped out of bed before Zack to go down to the barn to do the overseeing that she did every morning, making sure the Rocky D was ready for the day. Then...

She'd felt the slight cramping. She'd taken a break, gone to the bathroom and found...her period. She had to tell Zack, but she needed to absorb the idea of not being pregnant first...had to tamp down her disappointment that should have been relief.

She couldn't keep the questions from running through her head. After their loving last night, would

Zack still leave after New Year's? Would he ask her to go with him? *Could* she leave the Rocky D? But the one that bothered her most was the one concerning Zack and how he felt about marriage. She'd always dreamed of marriage and a family. She wanted them both together. She wanted to do it right.

But if Zack couldn't commit to forever...

She and Hank were saddling up two of the horses to exercise them in the arena when Zack came into the barn, his expression worried.

What she'd love was a morning kiss and a hug. What she'd like was to put her arms around Zack and ask him what was wrong. But with Hank standing there, they couldn't seem to be free with each other.

"Can you come up to the house?" Zack asked.

"Problem?" she inquired, knowing there was even before the question popped out.

"Dad wants to talk to us."

Hank took the horse's reins from her hands. "I'll take care of Jiggs."

With a "thanks," she reluctantly let go of the reins, then followed Zack. Once outside the arena, she stole a glance at him as they walked. "Is your dad okay?" *Are you okay?* she wanted to add.

"I'm not sure. He has this look of grim determination on his face and we're meeting in his study, so this is formal."

"He seemed quiet yesterday."

"I know. I was going to spend some time with him last night but—" He cut off abruptly.

But they'd met in the barn. They'd made love in the barn, and then all night long. Did Silas know they were together? Is that what this meeting was about? She was so aware of Zack beside her, his brooding intensity, his sheer physical presence. He hadn't worn a jacket. His thick, navy sweater made her want to burrow into his chest. His quick strides made her want to shout, *Stop, let's talk about last night.* His black hair blowing in the wind made her want to run her hand through it, not just for today, but for tomorrow and all the tomorrows to come. But Zack's tomorrows, at least for the next few months, consisted of traveling and interviews and production meetings and a movie he wanted to make. Where could she possibly fit into that?

Maybe he was wondering the same thing. Because suddenly, he wasn't on the move. He was stopping, stepping closer, sliding his hand under her hair, bringing her to him for a kiss. It was a long, heated, deep kiss that reminded her of the closeness they'd had last night. But then he was leaning away and saying, "Let's go find out what this meeting's about."

Silas sat in his wood-paneled study, not looking as imposing as he once did behind the huge mahogany desk. With a no-nonsense business look on his face, he motioned to the two leather club chairs.

"Have a seat," he said. "There's something I need to say to the both of you."

Jenny couldn't tell from Silas's expression or the way he looked at her and Zack what this was about. Over the years she'd had hundreds of meetings with Silas in this room. But none of them were quite as formidable as this one seemed to be. A chill ran up her spine and she wanted to take Zack's hand for support. But he stood ramrod straight, waiting for her to be seated before he was. She sank down onto the chair, rather wishing she could stand. Zack seemed to be feeling the same way because it took him a few moments before he lowered himself into the chair.

Silas folded his hands on the desk blotter, as if he needed some kind of calming gesture, too. Then he cleared his throat. Finally he said, "I've received an offer for the Rocky D that I have to consider."

Jenny felt a gasp escape her lips, as if she'd been punched in the solar plexus. Zack had gone motionless, just staring at Silas in silence.

"A businessman from Houston wants to develop the land into a retirement village."

Silas's words hung in the air and Jenny couldn't seem to find a response.

But Zack did. His voice tight, he said, "I didn't think you'd ever want to sell."

"I don't see that I have a choice." Silas sounded weary and defeated as he went on, "I can't act like an owner anymore, driving to sales, keeping up with the latest breeding techniques, training yearlings myself."

"That's nonsense!" Zack protested. "You're recovering from your heart attack. You can do whatever you want to do. You're still young." He said it forcefully, as if his energy could somehow instill in Silas hope for the future.

"Maybe I'm just plain tired. The doc says I should reduce stress. Maybe I want to slow down. Maybe the dreams I have for the future have nothing to do with the Rocky D."

"What are those dreams?" Zack asked, as if he had the right to know.

"I want to spend more time with Anna. I don't want to worry if we've got red ink on the books. I don't want to worry if I'm overburdening Jenny, or taking advantage of the hands, or simply not doing everything I need to do. That heart attack made me see everything in a different light."

His gaze came to rest affectionately on Jenny. "I'm not going to leave you out in the cold. I would never do that." He lifted a piece of paper from his desk and slid it across to her. "Brock Winchester owns a place near Sedona. His foreman is retiring. I told him about you and he's interested in bringing you in. You'll have to interview with him, but I don't think there's any doubt that he'll like your résumé."

Her résumé. Leaving the Rocky D...like this. Retirement cottages or condos sitting on the land she loved.

"You can't sell the ranch as it is? Where will the horses go? Songbird and Tattoo and Dusty?" she asked with real fear in her voice.

"To sell this place as it is would take too long. I'd need somebody with money to burn. Somebody who didn't want to turn the ranch into a breeding factory rather than the place it is. I'd rather find good homes for all the horses, or give them away, than see that happen. And Songbird is yours, wherever you go."

She supposed she would like to see all the horses placed in good homes, too, with people who would love them. But still—

Suddenly, the door chime reverberated through the house.

Silas stood. "I know I've given you both a lot to think about. We'll talk about this again in a few days. Mr. Lowery is going to fly up here next week and he can answer all your questions. We're thinking about making the transaction final by the end of March." Silas targeted Zack. "But with you leaving, I wanted him here before Christmas."

Martha came to Silas's study door and peeked in. "I don't want to interrupt, but Jenny and Zack, you have visitors. The Larson family is here."

Silas motioned Jenny and Zack out of the den. "Go on," he said. "We're done here for now."

Jenny still felt shell-shocked when she and Zack entered the living room and found Stan, Helen, Tanya and Michael waiting. Helen had called to cancel their lesson on Saturday because they were driving to Phoenix. The two adults looked uncomfortable, but the kids wore smiles.

"We didn't mean to intrude," Stan said right away. "But we wanted to say goodbye."

"We're moving tomorrow!" Michael announced, readjusting his backpack on his shoulders and approaching Zack. "Tanya and I are gonna have our own rooms and everything."

Stan added, "After we got to Phoenix, your friend, Mr. Barrett, showed us a few places he thought would be suitable. Once we really get on our feet again we'll look for a house. But in the meantime, we found a townhouse that will be perfect."

Helen crossed to Jenny and gave her a hug. "Thank you so much for everything you've done."

"I'm going to miss you," Jenny said, her voice catching. She was going to miss them, but she was going to miss so much more, too, if Silas sold the Rocky D. This family was heading toward their future, something better for all of them. But she didn't know what was ahead for her, and as she took a glance at Zack there were no answers there.

Obviously putting aside what Silas had told them—maybe it was easier for him than for her—Zack said to Michael and Tanya, "Come with me. I want to show you that project I was working on."

The two kids exchanged a glance and then grinned. "I thought you forgot," Michael whispered to Zack in an aside that Jenny could hear.

"Not a chance."

The two kids ran down the hall after him.

Jenny found out more about where the Larsons would be living. They really did seem happy as Stan slipped his arm around his wife's waist. "Mr. Barrett told us he went to school with both you and Mr. Decker. He seems like a great guy. I mean, he owns this construction company, yet he acted like I was his equal."

"Dawson remembers where he came from."

They were talking about everything the kids would love about Phoenix when Zack, Michael and Tanya came back into the room, Michael swinging his backpack happily. They all wore smiles, though now Zack's seemed a bit forced.

Ten minutes later, the Larsons were gone and it was just Zack and Jenny standing in the living room. "You did a wonderful thing for them," Jenny said again.

Zack was sober. "Michael and Tanya told me they're going to miss their friends, but then Michael added his parents have stopped fighting. That's huge for a kid."

She knew how huge that would have been for Zack. How his ideas of marriage would have been so different if his parents had had a different relationship.

Zack checked his watch as if the conversation had gotten too uncomfortable, or as if he wanted to shut it down before it did. "I have to make a few calls."

"Zack, we have to talk."

"I think we should wait until what Dad told us sinks in."

"It's already sunk in. If he does this, the Rocky D will be no more."

Zack's jaw tightened and his shoulders squared. "Don't you think I realize that? I grew up here, Jenny. I learned to ride here. I gentled my first horse here. I shot my first video here."

He'd first kissed her here, too. "Then you do care if he sells the ranch?"

"I care. But I don't know if that means anything to him. I don't know if it changes anything for me. Are you going to try to convince him not to sell?"

"Only *you* can do that. You're the heir."

"The heir? I haven't thought of myself as that for years. You're more of a daughter to him than I've ever been a son. If you want to stay, then you need to convince him not to sell. Here, you're like a daughter. Somewhere else you'll be an employee."

"Do you want me to convince him so you don't lose the Rocky D?"

When Zack didn't answer, she just shook her head. "You say you love traveling. But I'm not so sure you like wandering any more than I do. If the sale of the Rocky D bothers you, have you asked yourself why?"

"Memories of my mother are here," he said gruffly. "Memories of you and our friends are here. I hate to think we'll lose who we once were to a retirement village."

"Are you telling yourself you wouldn't feel as bad if Silas were selling the Rocky D as is to someone who wanted to keep it going?"

"It wouldn't be destroyed."

"No, but it would be changed. No one will handle the Rocky D like your dad."

"Before this visit I might have said that was a good thing. Now, I'm not so sure."

Jenny couldn't wait any longer to tell him what she needed to tell him but didn't want to tell him. "I'm not pregnant. I got my period."

Again he kept silent and Jenny knew Zack did that when he wanted to withdraw, when he didn't want to show anyone his feelings. He was so good at not showing anyone his feelings.

Finally, he said, "That's for the best."

His calm and stoicism lit her anger. "For the best? For who? For you? So you don't have to think about ties and commitment and what you really feel?"

His voice gentled as he asked, "Jenny, would you really want to have a baby this way?"

"What way? You mean without marriage? Without vows? Without a white dress and a picket fence? Maybe I'll take a baby any way I can get one. Maybe I want your baby more than I want anything. But you're leaving after the New Year and you're going to treat *us* like an affair that never should have happened. I get it, Zack. You just don't want the strings. Or if you want any strings, you want them to be all on your terms."

She felt tears pushing against her eyes and she would *not* cry in front of him. She *would not*. The idea of losing Zack's baby and the Rocky D all in one day was just too much. "I have work to do in the barn." She started for the door.

"Jenny."

But she couldn't turn back. She couldn't look at him

and not ache so deep down in her heart. She didn't know if she'd ever be without the pain again.

"Go make your calls, Zack. I'm going to spend as much time with the horses as I can, *while* I can."

Then she was through the kitchen and out the back door before Zack could come after her. There would be no point in him coming after her...because he simply didn't love her the way she loved him.

Zack had never felt so unsettled in his life. The foundation of his world seemed to be breaking apart and he didn't understand it one bit. His life wasn't here anymore, at the Rocky D. He'd been happy in California before he'd come.

Hadn't he?

Or had a sense of restlessness nagged at him often the past couple of years? Had he buried himself in his work because the rest of his life was so barren? When Jenny had revealed she wasn't pregnant, why had he suddenly felt the same way he had the night she'd told him about her miscarriage? Shaken up, different, wondering what his purpose was in being on this earth.

His movies had always been his purpose. If they weren't enough anymore—

He rambled through the ranch house, memories from his life here floating back in every room. Maybe he needed to purge himself of them. That was all. Then his father's selling the Rocky D wouldn't mean anything.

The house was large. As he stepped into each room, he let movies play in his mind—his mother telling him stories and reading him books, her joy in arranging fresh roses in each room, her care in choosing furniture, decorations and the menu Martha would make. He even remembered times when she and his father had their heads together over a magazine, when they'd held hands walking to the barn, when they'd gone riding together on moonlit nights. They'd once loved each other deeply. Maybe his father just hadn't known how to express it, or hadn't felt worthy of it. Maybe as he grew older, he grew more desperate to reclaim his youth. Zack didn't know when he had forgiven his father for his weaknesses. Maybe when he'd seen him lying in that hospital bed. Maybe when Jenny had pointed out his mother had made her own decisions and poor choices. Maybe when Zack realized his own life wasn't what he wanted it to be. Jenny had seemed to understand that. She seemed to understand his ties to the Rocky D were stronger than he ever imagined.

Where *would* she go if his father sold the Rocky D? To a ranch in Sedona? Would she come to California with him? Yet he didn't want her doing that by default. Had he wanted her to choose him over his father and the land she loved? Had he wanted her to choose him without conditions? Rambling from room to room only made the churning in his chest more tumultuous.

Maybe he needed a session with Dusty. Maybe he just needed to escape the claustrophobic feeling that seemed to be hemming him in.

Jenny was in the mares' barn when she heard a noise—a noise that didn't belong. At first she thought it was the wind or the door banging, maybe a branch dislodged from a tree that had blown against one of the buildings. But then she heard it again…and a chill shivered up her spine. She'd been grooming one of the mares, trying to calm her turmoil, trying to make decisions with her head, along with her heart.

But nothing was clear. Nothing felt right. So she'd gotten into the rhythm of brushing and just concentrated on that. Now she slipped out of the stall, latched the door and ran to the side entrance.

The pounding was louder and she knew exactly where it was coming from—hooves against a stall door. Without a thought for anything but Dusty, she ran to the rescue barn, letting the wind whip around her, under her vest. She was barely mindful of the snow beginning to fall. The temperature was supposed to plummet tonight, and with the wind chill... She suspected exactly what had happened. One of the hands had thought he was being kind and instead he'd caused a disaster. Dusty needed his freedom as well as kindness. Maybe that's why he and Zack understood each other so well.

The banging became louder, more desperate. Jenny was afraid for Dusty...afraid he would do irreparable damage to himself. He'd been hurt so badly in the past. She couldn't bear to see him hurt again.

As snowflakes settled on the arms of her sweater, she didn't think. She just felt for the horse and the panic that had probably overtaken him. Since Dusty had been going into his stall more often, one of the hands must have thought they'd do him a kindness and close him in there for the night against the cold, against the wind, against the snow. But Dusty was afraid to be closed in, afraid someone would hurt him while he was there.

Running into the barn, Jenny called Dusty's name. He was kicking the outside stall door with all of his frantic desperation.

Jenny knew she had to get to that outside door and

open it. Her boots sliding on the icy walkway, she rushed to the outside entrance to the corral and pushed open the door. She reached Dusty's outside stall door and called to him again as her fingers fumbled on the latch.

Then it was open. But the force of wrenching it free made her slip on a patch of snow. She groped for something to hold on to. There was nothing there. Her legs went out from under her and she fell as Dusty reared up, his hooves hovering over her.

Zack heard the banging as soon as he'd stepped outside the house. Jogging to the corral, he climbed the fence in time to see Jenny unlatch Dusty's stall door. His heart jumped into his throat as she slipped and fell. He'd never been so afraid in his entire life, never felt so helpless or powerless, never realized his whole life was wrapped around one blonde woman who had held his heart since high school.

"Jenny, *roll!* Oh, my God, roll!"

At the sound of Zack's voice, Dusty rotated on his hind legs. Zack's body thrummed with adrenaline and his thoughts skidded around his head until only one was very clear—if anything ever happened to Jenny his world would collapse. He raced to her, ready to protect her however he could.

Dusty's hooves hit the ground about a foot from Jenny's shoulder. As he galloped past them, Zack wrapped his arms around her, breathing hard, holding her close, so grateful for a second chance to do what he should have done fifteen years ago.

Jenny had held his heart all this time and now he wanted to hold hers. He wanted to keep her by his side for the rest of his life. In that one terrifying, unforgettable moment when Dusty had reared up, he'd known he deeply loved Jenny Farber. And he'd never love anyone else. At that moment he'd known all of his excuses, all of his pride, were simply defenses against being vulnerable.

Now, he'd never felt so vulnerable.

He pulled away, only far enough away to ask, "Are you okay? Are you hurt?"

"No," she said as breathless as he was, and he wondered if she could read in his eyes what he was feeling. Since he didn't know if she could, he had to make it clear.

He kissed her. With snow swirling around, with the wind blowing, he held her tight and let his lips and tongue tell her everything he didn't know if he could put into words.

But she pulled away, looked up at him and said, "I'm okay, Zack, really."

She sounded confused, maybe by everything that had happened, maybe by his kiss.

"I love you, Jenny."

Her eyes widened and he thought he heard a small gasp.

"When I saw you fall, when I thought of you getting hurt. When I even entertained the possibility I could lose you, I knew then I was being a stupid fool. I came home for the reunion because you called…because you said you needed me. But when I saw you, I couldn't forget what had happened, couldn't forgive, couldn't understand."

"I should have gone with you," she said. "I should have trusted you."

"You'd had no experience trusting a man's word. We were young. We didn't know where life was going to lead. And I shouldn't have been so full of myself as to expect you to run off with me. Not after the childhood you'd had."

"Zack, I loved you. I really did. When I lost your baby I didn't know if I'd ever get over it. I tried so hard to forget you. I tried so hard to build a life here without you. But when you came back, I really had no defenses. It didn't take me long to realize I'd fallen in love with you all over again."

"This time everything's going to be different," he told her. "I'm going to move my editing studio here. I'm going to convince Dad not to sell the Rocky D and let the two of us run it. I *do* want to continue to make movies and I'll have to be on location. But you can come with me if you want and I will always come home. Although I've tried to deny it all these years, Miners Bluff *is* my home. More important, *you* are my home. If Dad's determined to sell, I'll buy the ranch."

"Zack, are you sure? Because if you want to live in California, I'll go with you. I love you. You are my home, too."

"We have a lot of talking to do. We'll work it out. But whatever we decide, we'll be together. And not just together." He took her face between his palms. "Jenny Farber, will you marry me?"

"You said…"

"I said a lot of things. But now I'm feeling a lot more. I understand what vows mean. I understand the type of commitment you need. I need it, too. I want you to be my wife and I want to be your husband. And then I want to have lots of kids."

She was crying now, and he felt his throat tightening up and his eyes burning. Not from the cold, either, but from the emotion he'd been trying to deny for so long. He buried his nose in her hair. "I have to get you inside before you turn into an icicle."

She laughed and wrapped her arms around his neck. "Not before I give you an answer. I *will* marry you, Zack Decker. And I will always be your home."

He kissed her again as the snow swirled around them, as Dusty took another run around the corral, as their love enveloped them and Christmas bells jingled on the barn door.

Epilogue

Zack paced in his father's study, checking his watch. "He said he'd be here."

"The weather's bad, son. He might be having trouble on these roads. He still has half an hour."

This Christmas Eve, when his father called him "son," Zack felt like one. Maybe because he'd found the love he'd always needed, the love he never thought he'd have. Now, with Jenny's help, he'd found a different perspective on his father and on his childhood. He and his dad finally seemed to understand each other. After much discussion, he and Jenny had decided to live at the Rocky D most of the year and use his house in Malibu as a getaway. Silas could keep his hand in the ranch if he wanted, but he could retire if he didn't. The upside for him was that he could still live in the house on the land he loved, the house and land they all loved.

"This is why I didn't tell Jenny I called him. I didn't want her to be disappointed," Zack said.

"You did what you could. The rest was up to him."

There was commotion in the hall. Friends and family were arriving and taking seats in the living room where their wedding ceremony would take place. Mikala, Celeste and Abby were down the hall with Jenny, helping her get dressed.

Clay peered in the door of the study. "I think someone's here to see you."

Charlie Farber walked in, his suit a bit mussed and wrinkled, but presentable. "I got here as soon as I could," he said breathlessly. "The road from Sedona to Flagstaff was closed and I had to take the long way around." He went over to Zack and extended his hand. "I know I congratulated you on the phone, but I want to do it again. And I want to thank you for calling me. I know Jenny didn't because she didn't want to ask me to come and then be disappointed."

"You're here," Silas assured Charlie. "That's what matters. I offered to walk your daughter down the aisle when she told me she and Zack were getting married. But she's independent. She assured me she'd be giving herself away."

"I have no right to play any part in this," Charlie muttered. "I'll just be grateful if she doesn't throw me out. Can I see her now?"

"This way," Zack directed, leaving Silas's study and going down the hall with Charlie following.

Jenny was getting dressed in one of the spare bedrooms. When he knocked on the door, Celeste opened it, all smiles. "Hey, Zack. She's almost ready." Then she saw Charlie. She nodded her approval to Zack and called to Jenny, "Someone's here to see you. We'll be down the hall waiting for you." Zack had alerted Jenny's friends that Charlie might be coming.

Mikala exited the room along with Abby and Celeste, and Charlie went in.

One minute Jenny's bridesmaids had been flitting all around her, then the next—

She was facing her father. Her hand went to her mouth. "Daddy!"

"Hi, baby," he said approaching her. "You look beautiful. I've never seen a prettier bride."

Jenny had felt so special as soon as she'd tried on this gown. It was satin and lace with long sleeves, and a ruffled lace hem that fell into a train. Her headpiece was a very feminine version of a Stetson with tulle, lace flowers and beading.

Her father said, "I'd give you a hug but I don't want to mess you up."

Seeing his hesitancy, she hugged him, tears brimming in her eyes. "I'm so glad you decided to spend Christmas with us. I'm so glad you're here."

"I can't take credit on my own. Zack called me. He found me and told me about the wedding. I assured him nothing would keep me away. I haven't been a very good father to you, Jenny, but from the first time I saw you with Zack I knew there was something special between you—something special like your mom and I had."

"Will you stay for Christmas?"

"Aren't you and Zack going on a honeymoon?"

"We're not leaving until New Year's Eve. Everything happened so fast. We decided to stay and spend the holidays with Silas and our friends and then go to

Zack's condo in Vail. We didn't want to go too far away in case Silas needs us. How long can you stay?"

"As long as you want me here."

"You don't have to be somewhere?"

"Just here, seeing my girl get hitched. Silas tells me you're going to walk yourself down the aisle."

"I am."

"Good for you. Now I'd better get out there so I get a good seat."

"Since Zack called you, I'm sure he reserved you a place in the front row. Oh, Daddy, thank you for coming." She hugged him again.

When he kissed her on the cheek, he murmured, "Be happy, baby." Then in a stronger voice, he added, "You deserve it." He opened the door and stepped into the hall.

She'd hardly had time to recover from her surprise when Zack came in. "Are you okay?"

She and Zack had already agreed that they would make their own traditions and that his seeing her before the wedding wouldn't bring them anything but good luck. "I'm more than okay." She flung her arms around his neck. "Thank you. Every girl wants her dad at her wedding. And you've made it happen for me."

"I want to make a lot of things happen for you...for us. I have something for you."

"I don't need anything but your love."

The night Zack had proposed to her had been the most wonderful night of her life. He'd told her exactly how he felt that night. He'd risked his pride and made himself vulnerable. After he'd kissed her senseless, they'd checked on Dusty, making sure he hadn't hurt himself in his desperate attempt to escape his stall. In between making plans to get married, telling Silas and calling their friends, they'd checked on him. By morning he'd sought the shelter of the stall again, but this time with the door wide open.

Jenny loved the diamond she and Zack picked out together and the beautiful band that went with it. She couldn't imagine what Zack was bringing her now. He'd removed something from his inside tuxedo pocket. It was a velvet box.

When he opened the box, her breath caught. She recognized the beautiful pearls with the diamond and sapphire clasp. They had belonged to his mother. Tonight when she'd put on the pearl earrings Olivia had given her, she could feel Zack's mother's presence.

"My mother would want you to have these," he said. "Turn around and I'll put them on you."

Jenny turned and faced the mirror over the dresser. The pearls were a special wedding keepsake and she'd treasure them forever. The necklace meant the world to her and her eyes filled with tears again.

"Don't cry," Zack murmured as he secured the necklace and turned her into his arms.

"They're happy tears," she assured him.

Zack tipped up her chin. "I want to make you happy for the rest of our lives."

"And I want to do the same for you."

Zack's kiss spun her into a passion-filled future where their dreams would all come true.

* * * * *

Harlequin

COMING NEXT MONTH

Available October 25, 2011

SPECIAL EDITION

Harlequin® Special Edition® is thrilled to present a new installment in USA TODAY *bestselling author RaeAnne Thayne's reader-favorite miniseries,* THE COWBOYS OF COLD CREEK.

Join the excitement as we meet the Bowmans—four siblings who lost their parents but keep family ties alive in Pine Gulch. First up is Trace. Only two things get under this rugged lawman's skin: beautiful women and secrets. And in Rebecca Parsons, he finds both!

Read *on for a sneak peek of* ***CHRISTMAS IN COLD CREEK.***
Available November 2011 from Harlequin® Special Edition®.

On impulse, he unfolded himself from the bar stool. "Need a hand?"

"Thank you! I..." She lifted her gaze from the floor to his jeans and then raised her eyes. When she identified him her hazel eyes turned from grateful to unfriendly and cold, as if he'd somehow thrown the broken glasses at her head.

He also thought he saw a glimmer of panic in those interesting depths, which instantly stirred his curiosity like cream swirling through coffee.

"I've got it, Officer. Thank you." Her voice was several degrees colder than the whirl of sleet outside the windows.

Despite her protests, he knelt down beside her and began to pick up shards of broken glass. "No problem. Those trays can be slippery."

This close, he picked up the scent of her, something fresh and flowery that made him think of a mountain meadow on a July afternoon. She had a soft, lush mouth and for one brief, insane moment, he wanted to push aside that stray lock of hair slipping from her ponytail and taste her. Apparently he needed to spend a lot less time working and a great deal *more* time recreating with the opposite sex if he could have sudden random fantasies about a woman he wasn't even inclined to like, pretty or not.

"I'm Trace Bowman. You must be new in town."

She didn't answer immediately and he could almost see the wheels turning in her head. Why the hesitancy? And why that little hint of unease he could see clouding the edge of her gaze? His presence was obviously making her uncomfortable and Trace couldn't help wondering why.

"Yes. We've been here a few weeks."

"Well, I'm just up the road about four lots, in the white house with the cedar shake roof, if you or your daughter need anything." He smiled at her as he picked up the last shard of glass and set it on her tray.

Definitely a story there, he thought as she hurried away. He just might need to dig a little into her background to find out why someone with fine clothes and nice jewelry, and who so obviously didn't have experience as a waitress, would be here slinging hash at The Gulch. Was she running away from someone? A bad marriage?

So…Rebecca Parsons. Not Becky. An intriguing woman. It had been a long time since one of those had crossed his path here in Pine Gulch.

Trace won't rest until he finds out Rebecca's secret, but will he still have that same attraction to her once he does? Find out in CHRISTMAS IN COLD CREEK. Available November 2011 from Harlequin® Special Edition®.

Harlequin Super Romance®

*Discover a fresh, heartfelt new romance
from acclaimed author*

Sarah Mayberry

Businessman Flynn Randall's life is
complicated. So he doesn't need the
distraction of fun, spontaneous Mel Porter.
But he can't stop thinking about her. Maybe
he can handle one more complication....

All They Need

*Available November 8, 2011,
wherever books are sold!*

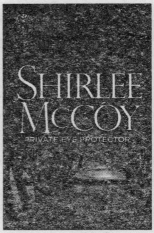

Harlequin®

ROMANTIC
SUSPENSE

CARLA CASSIDY
Cowboy's Triplet Trouble

Jake Johnson, the eldest of his triplet brothers, is stunned
when Grace Sinclair turns up on his family's ranch declaring
Jake's younger and irresponsible brother as the father of her
triplets. When Grace's life is threatened, Jake finds himself
fighting a powerful attraction and a need to **protect**. But as
the threats hit closer to home, Jake begins **to** wonder
if someone on the ranch is out to **kill Grace**....

A brand-new Top Secret Deliveries story!

Available in November wherever books are sold!